GUNMAN FROM RAWHIDE

GUNMAN FROM RAWHIDE

A WESTERN DUO

TODHUNTER BALLARD

WHEELER PUBLISHING
A part of Gale, Cengage Learning

GALE
CENGAGE Learning

Detroit • New York • San Francisco • New Haven, Conn • Waterville, Maine • London

GALE
CENGAGE Learning

Wheeler Publishing Large Print Western.
The text of this Large Print edition is unabridged.
Other aspects of the book may vary from the original edition.
Set in 16 pt. Plantin.

LIBRARY OF CONGRESS CATALOGING-IN-PUBLICATION DATA

Ballard, Todhunter, 1903–1980.
   Gunman from rawhide : a western duo / by Todhunter Ballard.
     p. cm. — (Wheeler Publishing large print western)
     ISBN-13: 978-1-4104-4296-3 (softcover)
     ISBN-10: 1-4104-4296-9 (softcover)
     1. Large type books. I. Ballard, Todhunter, 1903–1980. Dead men's
gold. II. Title.
   PS3503.A5575G86 2011b
   813'.52—dc22   2011031897

Published in 2011 by arrangement with Golden West Literary Agency.

Printed in the United States of America
1 2 3 4 5   15 14 13 12 11
FD302

ADDITIONAL COPYRIGHT INFORMATION

CONTENTS

DEAD MEN'S GOLD

I

Ken Gregory, special agent for the Texas Western Railroad, paused as he reached the edge of the crowd. "What's the excitement?" he asked.

A tall, lanky man in sweat-stained shirt and faded Levi's spat into the dust at Gregory's feet. "They're hanging a horse thief."

Reared in a country where a man's safety depended largely on his horse, Gregory instinctively hated a horse thief more than he did a murderer. He stared over the heads of the crowd to where the prisoner stood on a pile of ties, the rope already around his neck. Jed Dawson, obviously the leader of the hang mob, was talking to the prisoner, who Gregory recognized as a fellow named Sam Petnell.

Gregory saw Petnell arguing, then begging, while Dawson laughed. But suddenly there was an interruption, for a dark-haired girl had pushed her way through the crowd and was now facing Dawson.

"What are you up to now, Jed?" There was stinging contempt in her voice.

Dawson's leather-like cheeks flushed slightly, and his loose mouth opened with surprise. The prisoner brightened suddenly with renewed hope at sight of the girl.

"I didn't steal that cayuse, Mary. Jed just wants me dead. He knows that I know what he's up to." Petnell's eyes mocked Dawson. "He's afraid that I'll tell you. . . ."

"Shut up!" Dawson had recovered from his surprise and grasped the prisoner roughly as he faced the girl. "This ain't your affair, Miss Thorn," he said with mock courtesy. "I quit takin' orders from the Thorns when I quit the Box-T payroll. Sam here got excited a while back and took Ed Ross's horse. We're hanging him . . . the sheriff not being present to officiate."

"You're a liar." The girl's voice was low, but it carried to the back row of the crowd. "Sam Petnell never had the nerve to steal a horse and you know it. I don't know what this is all about, but I do know that you aren't going to hang Sam today or at anytime." She stepped forward and reached for the rope that bound Petnell's arms, but Dawson pushed her back.

"Take your hands off the lady." It was

Gregory who spoke now, and the crowd fell away from him as he stepped forward.

Dawson stared. It was the first time in the year that had gone by since he had been fired from the Box-T that any man in Ortman had dared to face him. His lips drew away from his yellow teeth in a sneering smile.

"Did you say something, stranger?"

Gregory ignored him. "Go ahead, miss. Take that rope off that poor devil's arms. Dawson won't bother you again."

Dawson swore. His body tensed as he leaned forward, and his hand swung stiffly at his side. Gregory gave no sign. His thumbs were hooked in his belt, and apparently his eyes were on the girl.

Suddenly Dawson straightened. As he did so, his hand swept up, bringing with it his Colt, but something was wrong. Before the long barrel had cleared the edge of the holster, Gregory's gun was spitting flame and smoke. A heavy slug caught Dawson's right shoulder, swinging him half around and knocking him to his back. His gun fell into the dust at his side. He attempted to grasp it with his uninjured left hand, but another bullet from Gregory's gun sent the weapon spinning beyond his reach.

The crowd stood silent, spellbound. The

13

action had taken place too rapidly for anyone to move out of the line of fire. Only two shots were fired. Dawson's gun had not burned powder.

The girl spent no time in surprise. She was at the prisoner's side in an instant, loosening his bonds. Then she stooped and caught up Dawson's gun. With it, she faced the crowd, standing fearlessly at Gregory's side. But no one showed any sign of hostility. The crowd fell away from before her, and she pushed the still frightened prisoner through the gap.

Up the main street of Ortman they went, the prisoner ahead, beside the girl. Gregory walked behind them, his own gun again in his holster, his manner unexcited by the mob behind him.

In front of the livery corral, the girl halted. "There are two Box-T horses in the stalls," she told Petnell. "Take the roan and ride out to the ranch. We'll see that you aren't hurt out there, and I'm anxious to know what you have to tell me."

He licked his dry lips. "It's about Will South's gold," he almost whispered. "I know where it is."

She stared at him. "You know where it is?" Her voice was tinged with disbelief.

He nodded, his hatchet face suddenly

cunning. "But I'm entitled to a share, ain't I?"

"Yes," she said with sudden decision. "If you find that gold for us, you get a third. Where is it hidden?"

He shook his head stubbornly. "I ain't telling you," he said. "But I'll show you at the ranch. That is, after you first get your brother to promise that I get my third."

"You'll get it." The girl's voice was beginning to show exasperation. "Now get that horse and ride. I've got to see Baxter before I start for the ranch."

Petnell went into the barn, reappearing a couple of minutes later, leading the roan. Gregory and the girl stood and watched him as he disappeared around the corner of a false-fronted building and took the north trail. Then the girl spoke. "I haven't thanked you yet," she said. "I'm Mary Thorn of the Box-T."

"My name's Gregory," he told her. "Ken Gregory."

Her face showed interest. "Not the Gregory that broke up the Roper gang . . . ?" Then, as she read confirmation in his face: "I've heard of you."

Gregory's face reddened beneath her gaze. "Shall I walk to the bank with you. I heard you say that you had to see Baxter."

"And you'll come to the ranch, too." Her tone was determined. She did not tell him that she was afraid to leave him in Ortman, afraid of what Jed Dawson's friends might attempt once they had had a chance to talk it over. "That's a fine way to ask you," she went on, with a laugh. "The truth is, I'm afraid to ride the trail alone after what happened this afternoon."

He nodded. If he guessed that she was lying in an effort to get him away from town, he gave no sign. "I'll be pleased to ride to the Box-T," he promised. "I have some things to do in Ortman, but they can wait."

The girl shivered. She guessed that the things of which he spoke concerned the crowd that was still standing about the fallen Dawson.

At the bank door Gregory hesitated, but the girl laid a hand on his arm. "Come on in. There isn't any reason why you shouldn't hear what I have to say to Case Baxter, and I want you to meet him. He was a friend of my father's, and he's about the only friend my brother and I have in Ortman. This town doesn't exactly like the Box-T."

She led the way past the cashier's window to the small railed-off space at the rear that served the bank president for an office. He was just entering this space as they stepped

16

into the bank, and he waited for them.

"What was all the excitement at the railroad, Mary?" he asked.

"Jed Dawson was trying to hang Sam Petnell," she told him.

The banker stared at her. He was a man of perhaps thirty-five or forty. Gregory could not be sure which. "Hang Sam?" he gasped. "What for?"

"Claimed that Petnell took a horse which didn't belong to him." Her voice was brisk. "Dawson was lying, and he knew that I knew it, but he wouldn't back down."

The banker still stared. "What happened?"

"Gregory, here, shot him," she explained. "Oh, Dawson's not dead, worse luck. Got a broken shoulder probably. But I sent Petnell to the ranch."

"You sent Petnell to the ranch? Why? Surely the Box-T doesn't owe Petnell anything after the way he quit you last summer?"

The girl shook her head. "I'd have sent him out, anyway," she said. "I'd protect a dog from Jed Dawson, but as it happens Petnell claims he has some information which I can use. He says that he knows where the Will South gold is hidden."

Gregory saw the banker's eyes flicker with surprise. "The Will South gold? Mary, you

17

don't believe that old story?"

"I'd like to," the girl told him frankly. "We could certainly use it now. That note we have with you, for one thing. . . ."

"About that note," Baxter interrupted her. "I've been meaning to ride out to the ranch, but I haven't had the chance."

She eyed him uncertainly as if fearing his answer. "It's all right, isn't it?"

"Oh, yes. It's all right." His voice was hurried as if he wished to reassure her as quickly as possible. "But with cattle prices the way they are and threatening to go lower, I've had to discount the note in Kansas City."

"You . . . you mean that you sold it!"

"There's nothing to worry about." His voice was still hurried. "As long as you keep up the interest payments, you're perfectly safe, but I wanted you to know."

"As long as we keep up the interest payments . . . ," she repeated slowly.

He stared at her. "There's nothing the matter at the ranch, is there, Mary?"

She shook her head. "Nothing much, except that for the last three nights men have been prowling around. We found their tracks. Last night Lefty Holmes caught them at it and got a bullet in the leg. I rode in for the doctor. I suppose he's at the ranch by now."

The banker said: "But who were they? What were they after? Surely not your horses?"

She shook her head. "That's what puzzled us," she admitted. Suddenly her expression changed. "I wonder, Case." There was excitement in her voice. "Maybe they were after Will South's gold, maybe there's some truth in Petnell's story. I'm going home and find out."

They had covered some ten miles of the winding trail before the girl slowed her mount. "I'm a fool," she told Ken Gregory. "If we keep this rate up much farther, our horses will never make the ranch, but I can hardly wait to hear Sam's story. Think of it. Ever since I was a child, I've heard about the gold that old Will South is supposed to have hidden at the ranch before he went East and never came back. Dick, that's my brother, and I used to dig for it every chance we got, but my father never believed the story."

"What was the story?" Gregory asked.

"About twenty years ago," she told him, "my father grubstaked a man named South. South was queer. Most people thought that he was crazy. My father did, I suspect, although he never said so. Well, one night, after everyone at the ranch was in bed, South rapped on my father's window. Dad got up and let him in. South was almost too excited to talk. 'I've found it, Bill,' he told Dad. 'I've found the biggest pocket I ever saw.'

"Dad was almost as excited as old South was. He asked where the pocket and the gold were, but South wouldn't tell. 'I brought it in a leather bag,' he said. 'I hid it here at the ranch house in a mighty safe place, and there it stays till I come back.' Well, that's about all there is to the story. Will South had a friend back East who he was going back to see. He borrowed a horse from Dad and rode to Ortman. There he took the stage, and that's the last that was ever heard of him in this country."

Gregory stared at her. "Maybe the old man never found any gold," he suggested. "Maybe he was crazy as you suggest, and only thought that he had found it."

The girl shook her head. "He had some with him when he got to Ortman," she returned. "The saloonkeeper weighed it up for him and gave him money in its place."

Gregory was silent for a while. "Maybe he took it all with him," he suggested finally, "and told your father that story about hiding it, merely so that he could borrow a horse."

The girl nodded. "That's what Father always thought," she admitted. "But now that this has cropped up about Petnell, I'm trying to make myself believe that there is gold hidden at the Box-T, and that Sam Petnell knows where it is. We certainly can use it. At any rate" — she went on with a laugh — "we'll know in another two hours. If I push the horses too hard again, tell me about it, Ken Gregory."

They rode on in silence, the country growing rougher as they progressed. In the west, the sun hung, a molten ball suspended above the purple hills. The trail was climbing steadily now, not a steep grade, but a gradual rise that made the horses labor slightly and slowed their pace. A line of hills grew on the right and the trail swung toward them.

Suddenly a rifle spat from the chaparral above their heads. Gregory's hat sailed from his head and lit in the brush a few yards distant, a little hole appearing as if by magic in its crown.

The girl reined her horse with an exclamation more of surprise than of fear. Another bullet whined above their heads, and a tiny puff of white smoke floated from the hillside to hang suspended in the lazy air.

Gregory was already out of his saddle, jerking the carbine from its boot as he touched the ground. "Get back!" he called to the girl. "Get back!"

She swung her horse about and it leaped forward on their back trail as the distant rifle spoke again. Gregory did not see her mount stagger. He was steadying his carbine on the distant smoke. It was a long shot for the short-barreled gun, but at least, he thought grimly, he could make the unknown bushwhacker uncomfortable.

Gregory fired again, with little hope that his shot would have effect. Then he turned his head to see the girl at his side.

"They got Baldy," she said, her face white and her eyes angry. There was a rifle in her hand. "That last shot got his head."

Gregory said nothing, but, reaching out, he took the rifle and handed her his shorter gun. "Stay here and keep shooting," he directed tensely. "I'm going to try to work around behind our friend." Then he was gone, disappearing into the brush.

The girl, following his orders, trained her gun on the distant hillside and fired regularly, but there were no more answering shots.

Quickly the conviction grew on Gregory

that the bushwhacker had gone. He quickened his pace, unmindful of the noise he now made. Suddenly he came upon a horse tethered to a bush. For a moment he stared at the brand on its side, a scrawling T set in a crude square. It puzzled him. Could one of the girl's own riders have been firing at them? Gregory pushed on.

Behind a screen of concealing bushes a man lay on his back. For an instant, Gregory believed that he had scored a lucky hit. Then he swore softly as he saw that the blood on the dead man's shirt was already congealed. He bent forward, then swore again. There might be gold hidden at the Box-T. They might even find it, but Sam Petnell would never have his third. For Sam Petnell lay on the ground before him — a bullet through his heart.

Gregory stepped backward, away from the dead man. In the surprise of discovery he had forgotten for the moment that the murderer might be lurking close at hand, waiting an opportunity to shoot. But nothing moved on the hillside, and, after a moment, Gregory continued his search.

A few feet beyond where Petnell lay, Gregory found the spot where the bushwhacker had been concealed. There were three empty shells and a burned-out cigarette butt close to the knee marks in the soft dirt. A trail led upward toward the top of the ridge. Gregory followed it rapidly, his eyes reading sign. He located the place where the murderer had left his horse, just across the top of the ridge. The ground on the far side fell away gradually toward the dry creekbed below.

Then something moved in the distance. Gregory shielded his eyes against the glare of the setting sun. The distant object was a man, a man on a pinto horse. Gregory felt sure that he would know the horse again. As he watched, the distant rider halted. It was obvious that he had seen Gregory, and he raised his arm and waved his rifle in a derisive gesture.

II

It was well after dark before Gregory, with the assistance of Dick Thorn, turned the tired horses into the Box-T corral. The girl had said little during the latter part of the ride. The death of Petnell did not weigh heavily upon her, but she was suffering from the anticlimax of the excitement.

Silently they consumed the supper that the cook set before them. Then the girl went up to relieve the doctor at the bedside of the wounded foreman. Dick Thorn led Gregory toward the bunkhouse. They stepped in through the door and the young cattleman waved toward the empty bunks.

"Sorry we can't offer you a bed in the house," he said, "but with Lefty in the spare room, there isn't any to offer. You'll have this to yourself. The boys are all up at the summer camp with the herd. We use the mountain meadows in summer and bring the cattle down to Thorn Valley for winter feed."

Gregory nodded. "Anything I can do to help?"

Young Thorn shook his head. "I'm sitting up," he said grimly. "I'd like nothing better than to get a shot at the coyotes that got Lefty, but I don't expect them back tonight." He went out, and Gregory threw his blankets onto a lower bunk.

Gregory awakened and rolled over. The room about him was still in darkness, but an oblong light appeared at one end where the open door showed the faint moonlight beyond. Gregory rose and dressed in the darkness, then stepped to the door. A man sat with his back to the bunkhouse wall, a rifle across his knees.

"Hello, Gregory. Come on out and sit

down." It was Dick Thorn, and he moved over on the low bench to make room for the railroad agent.

Gregory sat down and drew forth tobacco and papers. "Any luck?" His voice was low, as if he feared awakening the sleepers in the dark ranch house.

Thorn shook his head. "I didn't expect them tonight," he said, "but I thought I'd sit up for a while and see."

"Expect who?" Gregory had his cigarette going, and he was staring toward the corral.

Thorn hesitated. "I wish I knew," he admitted. "If you hadn't broken Dawson's shoulder, I'd think that it might have been him, but Petnell was killed after that. You didn't get a look at the man as he rode away, did you?"

Gregory said — "He was too far." — and let it go at that. "Think they're after the hidden gold?"

Thorn stretched his arms. "I don't know what to think," he said. "Dawson and Petnell used to ride for us when my father was alive. So did Red Zeller. I fired Dawson and Petnell, and Zeller quit. Dawson went into Ortman, taking Petnell with him. Zeller went over to the AC. Cowan gave him a job to spite me." There was anger in Thorn's short-clipped words.

Gregory asked: "Who's Cowan?"

"Bert Cowan. He's a range hog if there ever was one." Thorn's voice was tight. "His home ranch is in Grass Valley, thirty miles to the east, but his stock is on our range most of the time. He keeps nine riders regular, and there's always some grubliners hanging around. They're a tough outfit, and no one in the country has much to do with them."

"Do you think that Cowan is mixed up with Dawson?" Gregory asked.

"He gave Zeller a job," Thorn said, rising. Then his voice changed. "I'm going to turn in now. We won't have any callers this late. I haven't thanked you for what you did for my sister. I'm thanking you now. You're welcome at the Box-T any time. That is . . ." — there was bitterness again in his voice — "you're welcome as long as it's ours."

He was gone, stalking silently toward the house. Gregory watched him go, then went back to his bunk.

III

There was a horse beside the Box-T corral as Gregory rode up, a pinto horse that he eyed thoughtfully as he turned his own mount into the corral and walked toward

27

the house. It was a week since Petnell had been killed, and in that week the Box-T had not been troubled again by the night riders. Gregory had just ridden in from the summer camp with word for the cook that provisions were growing low.

Dick Thorn was not in evidence, but his sister was on the ranch house porch, talking to a stranger. She turned suddenly as she heard Gregory, and then relaxed, a smile showing about her full lips when she saw who it was. Gregory hesitated at the steps, but she motioned for him to come up.

"I want you to meet Bert Cowan," she said. "Bert, this is Ken Gregory."

The big man in the sweat-stained shirt offered his hand. "Glad to see you, Gregory. Mary was just telling me how you made Dawson crawl."

No surprise showed in Gregory's face as he shook hands, but he wondered what Cowan was doing at the Box-T. There was no enmity in Mary's eyes as she looked at the owner of the AC. In fact, there was something else, which made Gregory wonder. He thought of Dick Thorn's words — *Cowan is a range hog.* There had been anger in Thorn's voice, but it was more than evident that this feeling was not shared by Thorn's sister.

Cowan, however, seemed uneasy in Gregory's presence, and in a few moments decided to go. As he did so, there was the sound of horses from the trail behind the house, and Dick Thorn rode up to the corral with Case Baxter. Mary uttered an exclamation of surprise and dismay. Gregory, who was watching Cowan, saw him stiffen, then relax slightly.

Dick Thorn stared for a moment at the horse beside the fence, then dismounted, and, throwing the reins over his mount's head, walked purposefully toward the house. Case Baxter took his time. The banker did not seem anxious to be at hand for the outbreak that appeared imminent. Gregory backed against the porch rail and waited. This, he knew, was a private feud, one in which an outsider would not be welcome.

Thorn reached the porch steps and mounted slowly, never taking his eyes from the face of his unwelcome guest.

"Cowan!" His voice held a warning. He paused on the top step.

"Dick, stop it." The girl stepped between them, facing her brother, her face dead-white, her eyes angry. "This is my home as much as it is yours. If I choose to invite my friends here, I certainly do not expect them to be insulted."

Thorn reached out one hand and caught his sister's wrist. He pulled her toward him, and then pushed her toward Gregory. The railroad man caught her instinctively and stood, one arm on her shoulder, half screening her with his body.

"So you thought you'd come over and have a look at your new ranch," Thorn's voice rasped. "Well, it's not yours yet, Bert Cowan, and until it is, you're not wanted here, either in the daytime or at night."

The words brought a dull flush to the big man's face, but he stood silently, his arms crossed over his chest, his eyes not on Thorn, but beyond him.

"I can't draw on you," he said levelly. "You don't like me. Well, I can't help that, either." Gregory felt a sudden feeling of respect for Cowan. The man might be a murderer and a range hog, but he had complete control over himself. In comparison, Dick Thorn seemed like an angry, impetuous child.

"Get out!" Thorn's voice rose again. "And the next time you come, Cowan, come shooting. And have all your hired toughs at your back, for we'll be waiting for you. Now, get out!" Thorn turned and walked down the steps and around the corner of the house.

Cowan looked after him, amusement for

the moment twitching at his stern lips. Then he turned to the girl, who still stood at Gregory's side.

"I'm sorry this happened, Mary, but I blame neither you nor your brother." He walked away, striding past the banker with a curt nod, which Baxter returned.

"Bert, wait." Mary Thorn left Gregory's side and ran down the steps. She reached the corral just as Cowan swung into the saddle. For a moment they spoke together. Then Cowan raised his hand to his hat and, swinging his horse, rode off toward the east. The girl watched him for several moments, before she turned toward the house. Her brother reappeared just as she reached the steps, and she gave him a look of contempt.

"I hope you're satisfied. Bert Cowan came over to offer his help."

Thorn jeered. "Sure he came over to offer his help," he said. "Why shouldn't he? He figures that in another six months the Box-T will belong to him."

Something in her brother's voice quieted her anger. "Belong to him? I don't understand."

"Of course you don't." Thorn's voice was softer, kinder, and on impulse he slipped his hand about her shoulder. "You know that note of ours that Case was forced to discount in Kansas City? Well, Cowan bought it. The first time we miss an interest payment, the Box-T will be his."

Disbelief grew in the girl's eyes. "Bert Cowan did that?" She swung to the banker and read confirmation in his face.

"I'm sorry, Mary." The banker's face showed sympathy. "I was on my way out to tell you when I met Dick."

The girl nodded, her face set. For a moment she stared after the big figure disappearing down the AC trail, then turned and went into the house.

Case Baxter turned toward Thorn. "I guess you're right, Dick, but I never would have thought it of Mary." There was a tone in the banker's voice that made Gregory stare at the man's face. Then he turned away and walked toward the corral. He squatted on his heels beside the fence and waited until Case Baxter had mounted and left for town, then he rose and entered the bunkhouse, thinking.

Gregory was hunting gold, but his search was not a labored one. He sat on the shady side of the bunkhouse, his hat drawn well down over his eyes. The cook came out of the cook shack, stared at him for a moment, then, muttering to himself, gathered an arm load of wood and disappeared. It seemed to him that Gregory was the laziest grubliner he had seen in thirty years.

"That man don't do nothing but set in the shade." He poked the stove viciously. "If it was up to me, he'd work or he wouldn't eat."

Gregory, untroubled by the cook's wrath, continued to survey his surroundings. He didn't have time to dig, the railroad man mused. *Therefore he didn't dig. He hid it somewhere. The question is, what spot could he find where no one would be likely to stumble on it?* He brooded over the problem for almost an hour. Then, finding no answer, he rose, kicked the dust thoughtfully with his boot heel, and walked around the bunkhouse.

Things weren't running smoothly at the ranch. Mary barely spoke to her brother, and Dick Thorn carried a worried expression on his boyish face. Mary Thorn had come out onto the porch now, and Gregory turned and went toward her as she waved to him. Gregory saw that the girl's face was set, and that she held a white piece of paper in her hand.

"I wonder . . . ," she said as Gregory reached her side, "I wonder if you'd do a favor for me?"

33

Gregory nodded. "I'll be glad to, Miss Thorn."

She looked about nervously as she spoke, then turned toward the door. "Come in. I'm going to write a note and I want you to deliver it. I've no one else to send."

She looked at Gregory keenly, but there was no indication of his feelings in his face as he followed her through the doorway. She crossed the main room and opened a second door. Gregory followed her and peered about in surprise. It was a woman's room, its bed made and covered with a dark spread, but he sensed that it had not been used in a long time.

"My mother's room," the girl explained. "She died when I was born, and Dad kept it this way as long as he lived. I haven't had the heart to change it since." She seated herself at a small desk and, drawing forth pen and ink, began to write.

Gregory looked around. There was an open closet to the right, its entrance shielded by a curtain behind which he saw dresses. Beneath the window was a heavy chest, such as were brought across the plains by early-day immigrants.

The girl finished writing and folded her note. She rose and handed it to Gregory. "Give it to Bert Cowan," she said in a toneless voice. "Don't give it to anyone else. It's a long ride to the AC, but I have no one else to send."

Gregory nodded and tucked the note into his shirt pocket. Once on the trail, he put spurs to his horse and left the ranch house as quickly as possible, for he had no desire to meet Dick Thorn and be forced to explain what errand took him to the enemy's camp.

Ten miles from the Box-T Gregory halted his horse and stared thoughtfully at what lay ahead. "Horse," he said, rubbing his mount's neck beneath the mane, "I'm going to do a dirty trick, but when a nice girl like Mary Thorn writes notes to a man who rides a pinto, and a murderer rides the same horse, I kinda want to know what is falling out of the cards." He drew the note from his pocket and unfolded it. It bore neither address nor signature. The single line in the neat hand read: *Meet me at Salt Cañon, day after tomorrow.*

Gregory refolded the note and thoughtfully returned it to his pocket. The trail led almost directly through the rough country to the AC. But Gregory swung right on a side trail and rode ten miles out of his way to Millers.

There was nothing at Millers to attract the passer-by. Here were loading chutes and

35

here the AC shipped their stock, thus avoiding the long, dry drive to Ortman. A boxcar had been set off to one side to serve as a station, but there was no agent. Gregory pried open the door, seated himself before the telegraph instrument, and sent two messages. He waited idly for an hour until his answers came. Then, with a peculiar expression of satisfaction on his face, he returned to his horse.

The home ranch of the AC was a pretentious establishment. A hundred yards below the corrals was Grass Creek whose waters flowed on for another fifteen miles before they disappeared into the sand.

The grub call sounded as Gregory rode up to the corral, and the men were coming from the bunkhouse and barn as he dismounted. He made out Cowan's shoulders above the others.

The owner of the AC expressed no surprise at Gregory's presence, nor did he offer his hand. "Slim, take Gregory's horse. Supper's just ready. There's a pail of water at the bunkhouse."

When Gregory had washed, he found the men already seated. They paid scant attention to him as he took his place. He helped himself, and ate silently. Cowan sat with the men, and, when the meal was finished, he turned toward the door, motioning Gregory to follow. At the ranch house he lit a lamp and set it on the table, then faced his visitor.

"Well?"

Instead of answering, Gregory drew forth the note and handed it to the ranchman. Cowan took it slowly, unfolded it, and read it without comment, then looked up. "I don't know who you are," he said bluntly. "You're not an ordinary saddle tramp, looking for a job. I want to know what your game is?"

Gregory flushed. In a country where few questions are asked and a man's past is considered his own, Cowan's demand came as a surprise.

Gregory eyed him steadily. "It doesn't matter who I am," he said. "I brought that note, not as a favor to you, but as a favor to the sender. You don't owe me a thing, Cowan, and I'm going to make sure that I don't obligate myself to you." He swung on his heel and walked through the door.

At the corral, a red-headed man leaned against the fence. He eyed Gregory as Gregory passed, but the railroad man apparently did not see him. Gregory roped his tired horse, threw the saddle onto its back, and tightened the cinch. As he mounted, he heard a voice call — "Zeller!" — and he saw the man, near the corral, turn. Zeller was Dawson's side partner — Zeller was working for Cowan. The inference was clear, but Gregory was not one to make snap judgments.

Instead of taking the Box-T trail, however, he took the one that led to Millers. He spent the night wrapped in his saddle blanket beside the boxcar station, and, before it was light, he was busy at the telegraph instrument.

Evidently what he learned puzzled him for, as he mounted, his face was drawn in a questioning frown and, instead of turning toward the Box-T, he took the trail that followed the railroad track as far as Ortman.

IV

It was just growing dark when Ken Gregory crossed the street and stepped into the New York Saloon. He poured a drink from the bottle that the bartender shoved toward him, and then surveyed the room. At the other end of the bar, three cowpunchers wrangled among themselves. In the far corner, beneath a shaded lamp, six men played stud silently. Gregory watched them for a moment, then left the building. The bartender wiped the shiny bar top, and muttered to himself.

"Wonder what that guy's doing in town? I wonder if Dawson's pals know that he's here? When they find it out, we'll see some fireworks, and me with a new mirror." He paused in his labors and gazed fondly at his newest possession, which hung in a gilt frame above the low-backed bar.

Ken Gregory walked rapidly toward the hotel. He had ridden to Ortman to see Case Baxter, but at the bank they had informed him that the banker had left that morning for Kansas City. The thing to do, of course, was to wait for Baxter's return, but Gregory did not like to wait. There was one other possibility; he might hunt up Dawson and question the man.

The clerk was alone behind the box-like desk when Gregory reached the hotel. Through an open archway to the right a Chinaman could be seen, slowly clearing away the litter of the evening meal.

"Which room is Dawson's?" Gregory asked without formality.

The clerk stared at him, hesitating. It was evident that the clerk recognized him and did not know what to do.

Gregory's voice was soft, but warning.

"Don't hunt yourself trouble, mister. I asked which room Dawson is in?"

The clerk moistened his dry lips with the tip of his tongue. "Number Eight," he said. "Straight back, on your right."

Gregory did not give him a second look. He walked back through the dark hallway and pushed open the door of room Eight. The man on the bed looked at him in surprise, then swore softly.

Gregory said: "I want to talk to you, Dawson."

The wounded man stared at him. "I don't want to talk to you," he answered with an oath. "When I talk to you, I want a gun in my hand."

Gregory smiled faintly. "I'll be around when that time comes," he promised, "but right now you're going to answer some questions."

"Am I?" Dawson's eyes were mocking. "It depends on the questions, mister."

Gregory pulled a straight chair toward the edge of the bed. "I'm waiting to hear where that Will South gold is hidden."

Dawson's grin widened. "Heard about that, did you? Why not ask your friend, Petnell?"

"Petnell's dead," Gregory told him, and watched the other's eyes, but there was no surprise in them. Evidently Dawson had heard of Petnell's murder. "That's another thing I want to hear about." Gregory's voice tensed. "You're going to tell me who got Petnell and tried to bushwhack Miss Thorn and me."

"I ain't got a thing to say." Dawson's reply was complacent. "The only thing that makes me sore is the fact that the poor fool missed. If I'd been doing the shooting, you wouldn't be here now."

"Was it Zeller?" Gregory shot at him.

"Keep guessing. Maybe you're right, maybe you ain't."

Gregory rose, his voice tight. "Listen, Dawson. I've never taken advantage of a wounded man yet, but I don't figure that you're a man. You're a coyote, and anyone that does for a coyote is rendering a service to his community."

Fear leaped into Dawson's eyes. "Gimme a gun," he begged. "You can't do this, Gregory."

"Can't I?" A slight smile curved the railroad agent's lips. "Do you expect me to give a rattler the first bite? That's what you are, Dawson, a rattler. I give you just one more chance to talk. If you don't, I'll take you apart."

The man on the bed squirmed, then his

face relaxed. "I'll talk," he sneered. "It's too late for you to do anything, anyway. So what's the difference. By the time you could get to the Box-T, the gold will be gone."

"Gone?" Gregory stared at him.

There was a sneer on Dawson's face. "Yes, gone," he repeated. "We should have taken it a month ago, but Zeller never did have the nerve. The chief is running the show tonight. They'll take it quietly if they can, but they're going out there ready to fight."

"Where is it hidden?"

Dawson laughed. "In the simplest place in the world. There's a room at the Box-T that hasn't been touched for twenty years, the room where old Missus Thorn died. The gold is in that room, in a box under the window. Will South sneaked in there the night he left."

Gregory stared at Dawson. The man's tone carried conviction. Gregory knew instinctively that he was telling the truth. "How did you find this out?" he demanded.

Dawson was enjoying himself. He forgot his wounded shoulder, forgot that this man had threatened to kill him. "I picked up a bum in the New York Saloon a month ago," he explained. "This guy had been in some home for the indigent in the East. Will South was in the same home. He told this guy the story. When South died, the man started West to get the gold for himself."

"And what happened to him?"

Dawson's face twisted cruelly. "He died, I think."

Gregory started toward the bed, but a sudden noise in the hall made him turn. There was the sound of feet along the outside passage. Someone swore.

Dawson laughed from his place on the bed and raised his voice. "He's in here, boys! Have your guns ready!" A cry answered him.

Gregory's gun was in his hand. He started for the door, then hesitated. They needed him at the Box-T, needed him badly. He shoved the gun back into his holster and sprang toward the window. It was only a few feet above the ground, and in a moment he was on the sun-baked earth below.

A gun cracked from the building's corner, and a man came toward him in the darkness. Gregory fired at the gun flash and ducked sideways, just in time. Someone had reached the window from which he had just jumped and was firing into the darkness. A bullet plowed up dirt at Gregory's feet as he ran toward the livery corral.

A man at the corner of the corral snapped a shot at him. The bullet went through Gregory's shirt, between his arm and his side. He sprang forward, firing as he came, and the man went down with a startled cry.

There was a horse already saddled at the rack before the barn. Gregory jerked it loose and swung to its back, just as the men from the hotel came around the corner. A shotgun roared in the darkness, the pellets raining about Gregory, but the distance was too great for them to take effect. He was out on the north trail, urging his horse forward, before he realized that he had made a mistake. The animal was tired; it faltered. He was forced to slow his gait.

Gregory rode on more slowly now, watching his back trail as best he could, but there apparently was no sign of pursuit. This puzzled him. Why didn't Dawson's friends follow? With fresh horses, they would have had little difficulty in catching him.

The moon came up slowly, showing the dark peaks in the distance. Gregory's horse was laboring now. He swore and dismounted. The horse quivered, then stood still with drooping head. Gregory regarded it intently for a moment, then removed the saddle from its back and rubbed it down with handfuls of dry grass. That done, he seated himself and slowly built a cigarette.

It was almost 8:00 A.M. when Gregory rode

up to the Box-T. Dick Thorn came out to meet him, his face breaking into a welcoming grin. "I thought we had lost you," he said. Then, as he saw Gregory's bullet-torn shirt: "Hey, look's as if you'd had an argument with someone."

Gregory was staring about him. "Any more trouble with the night riders?" he questioned sharply.

Thorn nodded. "They were here last night," he said. "Shorty was supposed to be on guard, but he went to sleep. Still, he woke up in time and let out a yell. We drove them off."

Without answering, Gregory strode toward the ranch house. Thorn, puzzled, followed him. Gregory crossed the main room and opened the door that led to the bedroom that had belonged to Thorn's mother. The rancher started to speak, then checked himself, and stood in the doorway, watching Gregory.

Gregory paused before the chest beneath the window and raised the lid. A faint odor of lavender pervaded the room as he straightened.

Thorn said, from the doorway: "That chest hasn't been opened in twenty years." There was surprise and uncertainty in his voice.

"Hasn't it?" Gregory was looking down at the folded dresses in the chest. It was very evident that they had recently been disturbed. Suddenly he stooped and picked up a small object of dull metal. He turned with the pea-size nugget in his hand and held it out to Thorn. "Look's like Dawson told the truth," he said softly. "Shorty must have slept longer than he thought. Your visitors got Will South's gold."

Thorn's eyes were wide with incomprehension. "What are you talking about?"

Hastily Gregory explained. Then, suddenly, he broke off. "Where's your sister?" he demanded.

Again Thorn showed his surprise. "She went off riding early," he said. "I didn't ask her where she was going."

For answer, Gregory led the way toward the corral. The marks of the raiders' horses were plain. Gregory judged that there must have been at least six in the party. Suddenly he turned to Thorn. "Which way to Salt Cañon?"

The ranchman pointed in the direction in which the raiders' tracks led. "It's a wild spot," he said. "Do you think they headed that way?"

Gregory nodded, curtly. "Maybe. How many men have you got here?"

"Two besides the cook and Lefty Holmes," Thorn explained. "But Lefty is out of it, and so is the cook, for that matter. He got busted up some years back and can't ride. The rest of the boys are with the cows on the summer range."

"Get the two men," Gregory said, "and give me a fresh horse." He was already beside his saddle and shaking out his rope. "Which horse do I take?"

Thorn indicated a small buckskin close to the fence. "He's not much for looks, but he's good in rough country, and it's plenty rocky around Salt Cañon. It's just the place that Cowan would pick to hole up in, though why he shouldn't go on to the AC beats me."

Gregory did not take time to answer as he threw his saddle onto the horse. Five minutes later they were riding the Salt Cañon trail, Gregory in the lead, Thorn at his horse's flank, and two riders bringing up the rear. The young ranchman was still puzzled. He sensed that his sister was in some kind of danger, but he hardly knew what to expect.

They rode steadily, grimly silent in the periods when they paused to breathe the horses. The country was growing perceptibly rougher. Wind-carved cliffs encircled them.

47

Dry washes crossed their path. There were plenty of places for concealment, and Gregory's watchful eyes never left the trail ahead. Suddenly he pulled his horse to an abrupt halt. Thorn had difficulty in checking his mount in time, and cursed as the animal's feet slid in the gravel of the trail. Then above his voice rang the sharp report of a distant rifle.

"What is it?" Thorn was leaning forward in his saddle in an effort to see around the rocky abutment that jutted into the trail ahead of them.

"Seems like somebody's treed," Gregory said, slipping from his horse and pulling his rifle from the saddle boot. Together they advanced on foot, the two riders behind them. Just as they reached the rock, a rifle from the opposite side spoke, and a bullet cut viciously into the brush to their right.

V

Thorn grunted. "Rotten shooting." He threw his rifle to his shoulder, but Gregory stopped him.

"They aren't shooting at us. They haven't seen us yet."

"They're not? Who are they shooting at then?" The rancher lowered his rifle.

For answer, Gregory turned to the two riders. "Slip around to the left," he said. "See if you can get to the horses. If you do, stampede them."

Afterward, Gregory retraced his steps until the rock shoulder screened them from the cañon beyond. Then he started to climb, Thorn at his heels. From time to time, spasmodic firing told them that their quarry was still there and, after each burst, a lone rifle answered the outlaws from their side of the cañon. Suddenly, from almost directly above them, there was a sharp command.

Gregory's rifle dropped to the ground at his feet and he raised his hands, shoulder-high, palms outward. With a curse, Thorn followed his example, and a moment later Cowan stepped toward them, his rifle held ready.

"It didn't work, did it, Gregory?"

The railroad man regarded him, saying nothing, but Thorn demanded hotly: "Where's my sister? I might have known this was some of your work."

"My work!" Anger blazed in Cowan's eyes. "You're a fine one to talk, after sending Gregory to my ranch with a note in your sister's writing asking me to meet her here, and then trying to bushwhack me when I come along the trail."

Cowan's words carried conviction. It was not hard to see that his rage was genuine. Thorn turned to Gregory. "What is all this?"

"Cowan thinks that you planned to bushwhack him," Gregory explained. "I carried a note from your sister to him, asking that he meet her at Salt Cañon today. When he came, he ran into our friends."

"Are you trying to tell me that Bert Cowan and his men didn't get Will South's gold from the chest in my mother's room?" Thorn demanded.

"Some of his men did," Gregory admitted, "but Cowan wasn't in on the play. It was your friend, Case Baxter, that led them."

"Case Baxter? Are you crazy?"

"Hardly," Gregory told him. "If you'll dig around, you'll find that most of your troubles go back to Baxter. He wanted the Box-T, but he didn't dare move openly, so he sold your note in Kansas City, expecting the man to whom he sold it to foreclose. But Cowan's agent heard what was going on, and Cowan bought the ranch to save you. Isn't that right, Cowan?"

The owner of the AC said sharply: "Never mind that now. Where's your sister, Thorn?"

Dick Thorn looked first at Cowan, then at Gregory. "Have they got her? Has Baxter got her?"

"Yes. And we stand here like fools, talking!" Cowan swung about and started for the cañon.

Gregory caught his arm. "Hold on. I sent Thorn's men to stampede the horses. They won't hurt the girl."

Cowan shook himself loose. "To hell with you," he said, and was gone.

Thorn started after him, but Gregory stopped him. "Don't you be a fool, too," he said. "You can't get across that way. Stay here and keep shooting until Shorty gets the horses. We can't rush them."

Sanity returned to Thorn's eyes. "How'd you know about Baxter?"

"I telegraphed Kansas City," Gregory said curtly. "And that note Mary sent to Cowan, she was tricked into sending by Baxter. Damn . . . !" he bit off as firing broke out from the opposite slope. Throwing his rifle to his shoulder, Gregory answered the shots. There was no sign of Cowan in the brush below, but Gregory knew that the owner of the AC was making his way across the cañon.

"Stay here," Gregory ordered, "and keep shooting. I'm going to work my way across from above." Before Thorn could object, he was off, sliding through the brush.

As he reached the cañon's floor, shots broke out with renewed vigor, and Gregory swore, for he saw Cowan trying to rush the outlaws. Gregory felt a momentary admiration for the man. He saw Cowan break into the open and run across the intervening ground, unmindful of the bullets that flew about him. Suddenly Cowan paused, staggered, and went down. But he was up again, seeking cover behind a bulwark of rocks.

From where he now stood, Gregory could see that Baxter's men were entrenched on a small ledge just under the rim of the cañon wall. There was no way they could escape. In attempting to ambush Cowan as he rode down the trail, they had overplayed their hands — for his bullets had driven them back to the protection of the rocks. They could not climb higher. The only way of escape was to come out the way they had gone in. Thorn, across the cañon, was giving a good account of himself, keeping up a steady fire. Had it not been for Cowan, everything would have been perfect.

Soon he heard a shout. Shorty and the other rider had completed their circuit and had reached the cañon's rim, directly above the ledge.

Caught between the two fires, the outlaws stopped shooting, and a white shirt on the end of a gun barrel waved frantically. Gregory stood up and shouted: "Send Baxter and the girl down!"

A red-headed man stood up on the ledge. "They ain't here! Baxter's headed for the border!"

Gregory swore. "Come down with your hands up!" He stood, his rifle cradled in his arms, as they scrambled down, the fight gone out of them. He faced Zeller as the redhead reached the cañon floor.

"Which one of you rides a pinto horse?"

Zeller shrugged. "None of us. Baxter has one."

Gregory frowned. "So it was Baxter that killed Petnell." He cupped his hands and called to Shorty. "Anyone left up there?"

"Nary a one, boss."

Gregory cursed, his eyes on the prisoners until Thorn joined him.

"Baxter's headed for the border with your sister. I suppose he has the gold."

"What gold?" Zeller's red-rimmed eyes were questioning.

Gregory did not trouble to answer. He swung about. "Cowan!" He walked back toward where he had seen the rancher drop. "Cowan!"

A weak voice answered him. "Here."

Gregory climbed a pile of boulders, skirted

the edge of the wash until he found Cowan behind a pile of rocks on the opposite side, his shirt blood-soaked and his right leg useless.

"Did you find her?" was Cowan's first question.

Gregory shook his head. "Baxter is headed for the border with the girl and the gold."

"Damn the gold." Cowan attempted to drag himself upright, failed, and lay panting. "Go after them, man. What are you waiting for?"

Gregory paid no attention. He turned and called to Shorty for help, and, when the cowpuncher reached him, they packed Cowan back to the trail. The man was unconscious when they reached the rough track, and they laid him on the uneven ground. Gregory swung about to face Zeller. "Which trail did Baxter take?"

The man shrugged.

Gregory advanced a step. There was no questioning the menace in his eyes.

Zeller fumbled about for a moment. Then: "He went through the South Gap."

Thorn grabbed him by the collar.

"You're lying. No one would try the South Gap trail at this time of year."

Zeller shrugged. "Baxter did."

Gregory looked to Thorn. The Box-T

54

owner was shaking his head. "It's a hundred miles of dry trail, and, when I say dry, I mean dry. It's nothing but a burning waste. No horse can make it." He swung about as Shorty came up with the horses. "You get Cowan to the ranch," Thorn ordered. "Better take him to the AC. It's closer."

Gregory's voice was sharp. "You take him, Thorn. I'll go after them without your help."

The younger man's mouth was stubborn. "It's my fight."

Gregory's voice was tense. "Yes, but I've a better chance to get through. . . ."

Thorn stopped the argument by swinging his horse off down the trail.

Gregory swore, then jumped his own mount. "Shorty, it's up to you to get these men to the AC and take care of Cowan."

The cowpuncher nodded, bent forward over the wounded man, then straightened, his sun-scarred face very sober. "It's too late for Cowan." His voice was very sober. "He's dead."

Gregory stopped short. "Dead?" he repeated. Then with a curt nod he swung his horse and took the trail after Thorn.

As the miles slipped under his horse's hoofs, his mouth tightened into a narrow line. He hadn't sighted Thorn, or seen any sign of him.

The heat was growing more intense as he dropped down through the hills and came out on the level. He pulled his neck scarf up across his mouth and nostrils to cut out the choking dust. The sun was slanting down into the western sky. He gauged its height and slowed his pace. It would be cooler soon, and if his horse were fresh. . . .

Just at dark he came upon Thorn. The rancher's horse had fallen beside the trail, and Thorn sat beside it, his shoulders hunched. He straightened as Gregory stopped, rose, and came forward.

"Let me have your horse."

"And let you kill him?" Gregory shook his head. "Listen, Thorn. What little chance I have of catching Baxter before he hits the border is because I took my time. You're too anxious, you can't wait."

Thorn snatched at the reins, but the tired horse jumped sideways out of his reach. Gregory did not wait for more. He touched the animal with his spurs, and leaped forward, leaving Thorn cursing behind them.

It was daylight when Gregory saw, in the distance, two horses picketed beside the trail. His heart jumped. It couldn't be anyone else in this desolate sink. It had to be Baxter and the girl. He rode forward slowly, pulling the carbine from its boot as he came.

Hardly hoping that he could reach them without their awakening, he swung from his horse, dropped the reins over its head, and moved forward cautiously.

The first blanket contained the girl, and Gregory swore when he saw her, for she was gagged with her own scarf. The needless cruelty of it made him rage, but he did not have time to loosen her bonds. She was awake, and, when she saw him, her eyes moved as if she were trying to tell him something.

He nodded, and took a step toward the other blanket, then froze as a voice from behind him said: "Drop that gun, Gregory."

Gregory let the gun slide to the sand at his feet.

"Now drop the short gun."

Gregory drew the Colt from its holster, tempted to whirl and try for a shot, but it was as if Baxter had read his mind. "Drop it," he repeated,

The heavy gun slid from Gregory's fingers, and he raised his hands level with his shoulders, palms out.

Baxter came around a pile of boulders to the left, carrying his gun loosely. "Fooled you, huh?" There was a smile on his thin lips. He stood appraising Gregory in silence for several minutes. "Damn you. If it hadn't been for you, I'd have had the game my own way."

Gregory did not answer. He was studying the man, watching his chance. He knew that Baxter intended to kill him, but he wasn't thinking of himself. He was thinking of the girl. He said finally: "You might take that gag off her." He indicated the still form in the blanket. "I don't think anyone would hear her if she was to yell."

Baxter nodded. "I don't guess they would. Maybe I will." But he made no move toward the girl. Instead, his eyes remained on Gregory. "I hate to waste powder on you, *hombre*. Maybe you'd better start walking."

Gregory started with surprise. "You don't mean that."

The former banker grinned. "Ever seen a man lost in this sink, Gregory? They wander around and around, till they can't wander no more."

He turned and walked sideways toward the girl, still watching Gregory, his gun held ready. He dropped to one knee at her side and fumbled with his free hand at the knot behind her head, loosened it finally, and pulled the gag from her mouth. Then he

58

unrolled her from the blanket. Her arms were bound to her sides, but her legs had been held only by the blanket.

"You'd better start walking, Gregory."

Ken shrugged. "Better shoot me now, Baxter. It's easier that way. I've seen men die of thirst, and I don't care to."

Baxter's mouth tightened. "Well, you asked for it." The gun in his hand steadied. Gregory unconsciously steeled himself for the shock of the bullet

Then suddenly the girl's legs kicked out, knocking Baxter off balance. The gun exploded, kicking up sand beyond Gregory as he jumped forward, his arm swinging.

Baxter fired again, and the heavy bullet crashed into Gregory's left shoulder, half turning him around. But he came on, driving his right fist against the banker's jaw. The gun roared twice more, tearing at his side, but somehow he kept his feet. And his fingers were locked about Baxter's wrist, twisting it downward.

The banker still struggled, tried to free the gun, to bring it up against Gregory's side. It was coming up slowly. Gregory could feel his fingers slip from Baxter's wrist. It was only a matter of minutes, seconds almost. For one fleeting instant his eyes met those of the girl. They were wide, watching, unafraid. With the last of his strength he twisted just as the gun exploded.

For perhaps a second Gregory did not realize what had happened, why the man under him had relaxed so suddenly. Then slowly, painfully he managed to climb to his feet. Baxter was dead. The bullet had gone into his right side and torn its way out under the left armpit.

Stupidly Gregory looked down at the dead man. Then he turned and walked unsteadily toward the girl. He had trouble with the knots that bound her arms. The fingers of his good hand seemed stiff, and there were little black spots dancing before his eyes. He got the ropes loosened somehow, straightened, and stood swaying. The desert floor revolved in eddying circles about him.

Mary Thorn was ripping the shirt away from his arm, exposing the shoulder. Little beads of moisture dotted Gregory's forehead, but his lips remained tight pressed. The girl said: "Can you ride?"

He nodded weakly. "Sure." He knew that she was going for the horses, knew vaguely that he had to ride, that if he stayed here. . . .

He was in the saddle, somehow. The girl

was lifting a sack to the back of Baxter's horse.

He said: "Will South's gold?"

She nodded, and there was a little catch in her voice. "Now we can pay Bert Cowan."

Cowan — he'd forgotten about Cowan. He wondered if he should tell her that Cowan was dead. He decided not to. The trip ahead would be hard enough.

The sun, a red ball, climbed higher in the cloudless sky. Its glare blinded Gregory, dazed him. He had no idea of how long they had been riding. His arm was stiff and his side burned dully. Three times the girl raised the canteen to his thickening lips, but he pushed it away. They would need the water later, need it badly. He had to keep on. He didn't care for himself. He was past caring, but he knew that the girl would never go on without him.

And then there was a cry. Mary was riding ahead, leading Baxter's horse. Gregory could see the slim, tired figure straighten in the saddle. He tried to shout, knowing that his voice was little more than a whisper: "What is it?"

She said: "Riders. It must be my brother and the boys. Maybe Bert Cowan is with them."

Gregory never remembered afterward why

he said it. He thought it was because he wanted her to know, while she was alone, while she would have a chance to mask her grief. He said: "I'm sorry."

She turned in her saddle. "You're sorry. What is it? Tell me, Ken."

He could no longer see her distinctly. He had to steady himself with one hand on the high horn. He said: "I'm sorry, Mary, but Cowan isn't with them. Cowan can't be with them, you see. . . ."

She had stopped her horse and twisted in the saddle to look at Gregory. "You mean he's dead?"

Gregory nodded.

"Why didn't you tell me?"

A red glow crept up under the tan of his cheeks. "Well, you see, I figured. . . ."

"You thought I loved him?" Her voice had grown very soft.

He nodded, and suddenly slumped sideways in the saddle.

In an instant Mary was on the ground, running toward his side. Her arms were about his shoulders, pillowing his head. "Ken, oh, Ken! You can't die! You can't! You thought I was in love with Bert. I might have been once, but . . . but can't you understand? You can't die. You've got to live, for me."

He wasn't certain that he heard. He thought that perhaps he was dreaming. But he wasn't. It was real. The girl was sitting in the sand beside the trail, holding the canteen to his cracked lips. She did not look up until the riders reached her. Then she smiled. Everything was all right.

■ ■ ■ ■

GUNMAN FROM RAWHIDE

■ ■ ■ ■

I

Ray Donovan sang softly under his breath as he drove the rented buckboard over the dried ruts of the ranch road. He sang not from happiness, or from any feeling of satisfaction at being this near to home. He sang only from habit. It was a habit he had picked up following the long, lonely trails of the past six years. It helped to bridge the distances he had covered, helped to crowd down the loneliness that at times threatened to swallow him.

The road unwound ahead of him like an uncoiling snake, climbing the slopes of the wooded hills, sheering off at sharp turns to follow the lines of the twisting cañons. It was a high country, a country of rich mountain meadows, of aspen and pine, a land that was friendly in summer, but bitter and forbidding for both men and animals when the blizzards howled down from the heights.

It was spring now, and the air held its first

softness, and the grass of the meadows was turning green under the mats of ground-cured hay, and here and there flowers added their coloring, dainty and beautiful, as if they had been carefully placed by some artist's sensitive fingers.

Ray Donovan felt the beauty, and the lift in the air, and would not heed it. There was a grimness in him that refused to admit that anything about this land could be good. He stared straight ahead, humming his tuneless melody until the road made its final twist and fell away over the rim of the last ridge, and the trees thinned to let him have his first clear look at the valley below, at the high, box-like walls, the rough, weathered buildings, the fences and the corral that was the Box D.

He halted the rented horses, puffing now from their steady climb. Holding the reins in one hand, he put the other on the shoulder of the man who dozed at his side in the buggy.

"Come on, Bert." His tone was not gentle. "Wake up and begin to think of excuses. You're home."

Bert Donovan opened his eyes, rubbed across them with the back of a thick hand, and yawned widely. He stared at the buildings beyond them with no apparent pleasure.

"I'll give you a hundred dollars," he said, "if you turn around and drive back to Dondaro."

"No." There was the trace of a wicked grin in Ray Donovan's blue eyes. "Not for a thousand. I can't wait until the rawhiding starts. The thought is worth the whole trip."

"You're a bastard," Bert Donovan said, without ill feeling. "Come on, then. Let's get it over with." He was young, but already his good-humored face showed the traces of hard living. Likable but easy going, he was nothing like his older brother John.

Ray thought that most of Bert's troubles stemmed from the younger man's easy acceptance of life. Bert had never exerted himself to do anything, and Kate Donovan had never made him. Kate had always loved Bert the best, and being a strong-willed woman it was surprising that she had not managed to mold him into a pattern of her choosing.

Thinking about it as he started the team downgrade, Ray decided he was not surprised that Bert had run away; certainly he had felt no real surprise at finding Bert in the Denver saloon. His only surprise was at himself for troubling to force Bert to come home.

True, his action had been prompted in part by Marty's letter that had finally caught up with him the week before he ran into Bert. Marty had written:

I don't like the way things are going here at the ranch. Aunt Kate is not well, and she grieves because Bert ignores her pleas to come home. He's in Denver somewhere, been gone four months now, and there is no way of telling what kind of trouble he has gotten into by this time. If you should see him, ask him for me, please to come back. . . .

He had chuckled over the letter. He remembered Marty as a serious-eyed twelve-year-old who could ride better than most members of the crew, a wild kid who spent more time on a horse, roaming the hills, than she did in Aunt Kate's kitchen.

Ray was no relation to Marty. For that matter, he was no relation to any of them. But Kate Donovan's brother had pulled him out of a burned-out wagon train while he was still too young to talk, had given him his name, and raised him until he was nine.

Ray had found Bert before the faro bank

in the Silver Dollar, drunk and surrounded by dance-hall girls. He had hauled Bert up to his room, sobered him, and showed him Marty's letter. Bert had grumbled and protested.

"Why should I go back to that prison?" Bert had demanded. "The old lady gives me hell constantly, John preaches about the evil of my ways, and Marty looks at me like a dying calf I've betrayed. You don't know what I've had to put up with." He was feeling very sorry for himself.

"You're going back," Ray had told him, "if I have to hog-tie you and deliver you trussed up."

Bert had grinned wryly. "You'll have to do just that. I wouldn't think you'd feel any loyalty to Aunt Kate after the way she threw you out."

He felt no loyalty to Kate, no loyalty to any of the Donovans. There had been four of them originally, but Kate's three brothers had not taken to ranch life.

It was Kate who had stayed on the ranch with after their father's death, Kate who had raised her brother Frank's two boys, and her brother Albert's granddaughter Marty after both Frank and Albert were killed in a stage accident.

Pete Donovan had been the black sheep

of the family. Pete had preferred prospecting to working the ranch, or working in his brother's bank. Pete had roamed the West, and after he had found the baby boy in the burned wagon train, he took Ray with him, moving always from one mining strike to the next.

But when Ray was nine the tunnel in which Pete was mucking had collapsed, breaking Pete's back. He lived two weeks afterward, long enough to write to his sister, long enough to have his adopted son sent to the ranch.

Ray had found the other two boys already there, and the baby girl Martha, called Marty. He knew in some obscure way that John and Bert were brothers, and that Marty was their cousin. For nine years he had looked on all of them as his own cousins, and Kate Donovan as his aunt.

The Box D was his home, and Ray Donovan his name. It was the only name he had ever known.

He was eighteen the morning he licked John, and John was two years older. They had fought before, because John had a nasty way of ordering the other children around, but this was the first time he had beaten the older boy.

He remembered it all vividly as he headed

the team toward the gate that opened into the ranch yard. He'd had John down, against the corral fence, and he was battering at the older boy with a broken wheel spoke when Aunt Kate's whip curled about his shoulders.

He had jumped up then, trying to avoid the cracking lash. But it wasn't the burn of the welts across his shoulders he remembered now; it was the taunt in Kate's voice, calling him a brush bastard before the watching crew, a nameless, shameless, murdering sneak.

No, he did not owe Kate Donovan loyalty. He had crept away, hiding in the hay shed until after dark, then taking a horse and riding out. He had sent the horse back from Dondaro, although it was supposed to be his. He had caught it on the range and broken it, but he wanted nothing that was associated with the Box D.

He might have changed his name, but the name had belonged to Pete Donovan, too. Pete had given it to him, and he had loved Pete as he might have loved his own father. He had kept the name, and in a small way he had made it famous throughout the West.

He could have turned outlaw; he'd been bitter enough at the moment to try anything. But by accident he fell in with a railroad construction crew. Before the job was finished he had become a kind of trouble-shooter, working for the big bosses, policing the tough head-of-rail camps.

He was not a gunman in the accepted sense of the word, but since then he had bossed other crews, other camps, making his headquarters in Denver when he was not working, and remaining always a lonely man with many acquaintances and few friends.

The crews called him Tough Donovan behind his back, and threatened to get him when the job was done. None had, but several had tried. At twenty-four, he was a man whose reputation caused people to stop talking and turn to watch him when he entered a Denver saloon. No one argued with him, no one ever asked him to sit in a poker game, and no dance-hall girl tried to wangle a free drink. A hard, silent man, Tough Donovan. When he smiled, it was with mockery; when he laughed, people got out of his way.

The rented team came into the Box D yard at a high run. It was his way of showing his defiance to the woman who owned the ranch, for Kate Donovan could never stand to see a lathered horse.

He pulled the team up short, close to the

porch of the main house. Bert gave him a mirthless grin before he stepped down over the low front wheel, saying in an undertone: "You're really out to rile Kate, aren't you?"

Donovan paid no attention. The house door had swung open. Kate Donovan stepped out on the porch, followed by a tall girl who must be Marty.

John Donovan came from the blacksmith shop beyond the hay sheds and hurried forward, his sleeves rolled up to show the knotted muscles of his big forearms. Like all of his breed John was big and opinionated and hard. At twenty he had managed to force out the regular foreman and take over the crew. Since then he had ruled them with an iron hand, bowing only to his aunt's dictates.

But it was not John who held Ray's attention. It was Kate. On impulse he had brought her nephew home, merely for the expected pleasure of watching her anger, and he studied her now with narrowing interest.

Martha Donovan had seen Bert. She uttered a little cry of welcome, sped by her aunt, and ran across the yard to throw herself into Bert's arms.

"You're home," she said, and she seemed to be laughing and crying at the same time.

"You've come home at last."

Bert was laughing, too. He swung her off the ground and pivoted, holding her light body easily. "I swear, Marty, you get prettier every day you live."

On the buckboard seat, Ray felt again the knife-keen pang of loneliness, the hurt of being shut out, of not belonging, here or anywhere else.

And then Kate strode toward the buckboard. He saw the anger mirrored on her leathery face and forgot everything else. She had not changed. She looked no older than she had on the day he had run away. For that matter, she looked no older than she had on the day he had first come to the ranch, thirteen years ago. There was something ageless about Kate Donovan, something timeless, like the bare rocks of the high mountains to the north.

She was very tall for a woman, almost six feet. She weighed nearly two hundred pounds, but her big body was as tough as a man's and she carried herself proudly erect.

Her gray eyes were as hard and depthless as stone, her skin weathered until it resembled cordovan leather. Her jaw was square and her nose a high-bridged beak, and the mouth beneath the nose was a long, hard, straight line.

Imperiously she wore a divided skirt of fine black serge, a starched white shirtwaist caught at the chin-tall neck by a single large amethyst.

She wasted no time on Bert Donovan. If she were glad to see her younger nephew return, she kept the feeling well hidden. She walked directly toward the buckboard where Ray was fastening the reins around the whip in the socket, preparing to step out, and she told him in the flat, expressionless voice that was nearly metallic: "Don't bother. You aren't welcome on the Box D, Tough Donovan."

He stared at her in surprise. He had not expected a warm welcome, but he had expected some kind of thanks for fetching Bert home. He stayed his hand in the air, still holding the reins.

"You aren't welcome," she repeated, looking up directly into his blue eyes. "The next time I see you on this ranch I'll shoot you."

He said nothing. There was nothing he could say. All other action in the yard had ceased. Kate Donovan, as always, held the center of the stage. "You thought you could sneak back here without my knowing you were with the railroad," she added. "You thought you could worm your way into my good graces by bringing Bert home. Well, you can't. I'm on to you, and to your thieving bosses. Get out."

It was on the tip of his tongue to protest, to tell her that he did not know what she was talking about, that at the moment he was not working for the railroad or for anyone else. But he did not speak. All his old resentment, all his old hate of this woman rose up to choke him. Without a word he shook the lines, stirring the tired horses into motion, swinging the buckboard in a wide circle toward the gate.

From the corner of his eye he saw someone cutting across the yard swiftly. He heard Marty call his name. She was trying to catch him before he reached the gate.

He checked the horses and she came up behind him, catching the back of the seat and leaping lightly up, one foot on the small boot. The next minute she was at his side, a little breathless.

She leaned over and put one hand on his arm. The hand was long and slim, and brown from the sun. He looked at her and realized with a start that she was no longer the little girl to whom he had written through the long lonely years. For some reason that was not quite clear it had never occurred to him that Marty Donovan had been growing up. In his mind's eye he had pictured her as the little girl she had been on the day when he had fled from the ranch. She wasn't. She was eighteen now, a woman, a good-looking woman with her clear skin and clearer gray eyes that met his so levelly.

"Ray," she said, "I'm sorry. I shouldn't have asked you to bring Bert home. I didn't realize how it would be. I didn't realize what Kate would think. But don't leave Dondaro until I can talk to you."

She was gone then, jumping to the ground, and waving her arms at the team so that they spooked out of the gate despite their tiredness. He looked back, seeing her standing there, slim, and straight, not waving, just watching him.

II

Dondaro had not changed. Dondaro would never really change. It was of the country, rooted deep in a civilization that was old before the Pilgrims landed on the coast of a place they named New England.

The Indians loafing before the livery stable, the Spanish-speaking people with their blanket looms, the saloons and the dance halls, the big general stores, the stage station, and the three hotels — these were Dondaro.

Once he had thought that this was one of the important towns of the world, for his perspective then had been very limited. Now, looking at it against the background of experience, he saw it for what it was — a hill town, a cattle town, off the beaten track, its old false-fronted buildings a little tired.

The main hotel was even worse than he remembered it. Joe Stivers stood behind the high desk, chewing his frayed toothpick and giving his twisted smile.

"Never expected to see you in this town again. Come in to help with the railroad?"

He looked at the hotelkeeper carefully. Kate Donovan had mentioned a railroad; now Stivers seemed to think that he knew about it, was here perhaps to build it.

"What railroad?" he said.

Stivers grinned. He had a long nose, and he rubbed one side of it with a dirty finger. "You're a cute one, Ray. Heard about you, the way you handled construction, up in Wyoming. Well, don't tell an old friend about it if you don't want to. Take Number Five."

The words annoyed Ray Donovan. He had never been a friend of Stivers. He had never acquired many friends in this sun-baked town. He had been eighteen years old when he left, a rider off the range, one of the Donovan kids who rode into town on Saturday nights and made life miserable for the authorities.

No, he had never been a friend of Stivers. To the devil with Stivers, and with the town, and with Kate Donovan. Let them think what they wanted.

He took the key and climbed the stairs and went along the hall to the end room. Inside, it was hot. He pushed up the window, using the stick left there for the purpose to prop it in place. The air was stale. The bed was old, the thin mattress sagging hopelessly in the middle.

But he did not care about the bed. He had no intention of remaining in Dondaro. He would be here only until the evening stage pulled out at 8:00. He stripped off his shirt, slopped some tepid water from the flowered pitcher into the cracked bowl, and scrubbed himself free of the grime with which the three-day journey had coated him.

He thought of Bert and grinned sourly. He wondered how Bert was faring at the ranch. He wondered what Kate Donovan had said, and he wondered how long it would be before Bert chose to run away again.

He didn't care. He kept telling himself that he did not care. To hell with the Donovans, and all their relations. To hell with Marty, too. Not that he had anything against the kid. She had written him faithfully, all these years, every letter a friendly thing, telling him about the cattle and the horses, and the country he had once loved. Never a mention of herself, or of the other members of the family. It was as if she had realized how he felt without being told, as if she had sensed that he wanted nothing further to do with the Donovans. Not until the letter asking him to bring home Bert had she ever mentioned any of the family.

He finished sponging himself, drew clean clothes from his war bag, and felt better after he had dressed. He stretched himself upon the lumpy bed and lay, staring at the yellow ceiling without actually seeing it.

Was somebody actually thinking of building a railroad into Dondaro? It was possible, but it did not seem to make a great deal of sense. The country was too thinly settled. This was not the flat lands where already the hoe men were beginning to grow wheat. This was ranch country. Oh, there were patches of corn along the creeks, and a man could raise fine hay for winter feed in the mountain meadows, but there was not enough produce to support a line, and he doubted that there ever would be one.

A noise at the door made him turn his head. He saw Marty standing in the entrance. He had not expected that she would come. He had not thought Kate Donovan would allow her to come.

He said, a little mockingly: "Don't you ever knock before coming into a man's room?"

She flushed, the color climbing under the smooth golden tan of her face. Her eyes looked very gray and large and once again the fact struck him forcibly — here was a woman, full-grown and desirable.

Donovan had known few women. The ones he'd met around the construction camps had attempted to market what little prettiness they possessed. But this girl was very different. There was a proud honesty about her, a candid trustfulness. Here was someone a man could tie to, a girl with whom he could build a perfect life. He experienced a sudden sharp jealousy of Bert, and his smile became a little fixed as he attempted to hide the surge of his emotions.

"I didn't knock," she said, "because I slipped in without Stivers seeing me. This town is a gossip sounding board, but I had to see you."

"Why?" The stiffness was still in his lips,

making his voice a little unnatural.

She came in then, shutting the door. "You've changed, Ray." She said it as if in surprise.

"Of course. Everyone changes." He swung his long legs off the bed and sat up, watching her.

"You've grown bitter," she told him, "and hard. I'm not certain I like you as well as I used to."

He forced a laugh. She had all the appearance of a grown woman, but in some ways she was still as simple and direct as a child.

"Stay that way, Marty," he said, and stood up.

She looked at him, not understanding what he meant; then she remembered why she had come and asked directly: "Did you come back here to build this railroad?"

The question caught him off guard. He had forgotten about the railroad. His mind had been fully occupied with the amazing change in her, and with this new feeling for her that had flashed into sudden life, like powder ignited by a spark.

"Railroad?" He had to think for a moment to know what she meant. Then he shook his head, smiling. "I didn't, Marty. I never even heard of the railroad until two hours ago."

She sighed in relief. "I'm glad. I couldn't

be happy, thinking you were fighting Aunt Kate. She's certain you've come here to build that road, and that you only brought Bert home as an excuse to get on the ranch."

He laughed mirthlessly. "What Kate Donovan thinks doesn't worry me."

"And you aren't going to stay?"

"I'm leaving on the evening stage. But one thing I don't understand. If someone is fool enough to build a road in here, why should Kate be opposed? I'd think that the Box D would be the first to benefit."

"Would you?" she said. "The charter which the railroad company got from the federal government calls for them to receive from the government alternate land sections all along their right of way as soon as the rails are laid. The railroad is to come directly through the ranch . . . and, as you know, ninety percent of our grazing land is government owned. All we own is the water holes."

He understood at once.

"If the railroad is built," she went on, "over half of the ranch will automatically become the property of the promoters."

He was thoughtful. "And who are the promoters?"

She shook her head. "We don't know all of them. Wilbur Keats is their front man here. Kate has threatened to shoot Keats on sight. She's already run off two surveying crews."

"It sounds," he said, "like a swell fight."

Her mouth tightened. "I don't like fights, but I'm with Aunt Kate on this. We can't let them ruin the Box D. That's the reason I wanted Bert home. John won't help. John says we can't stand in the way of progress. John says we'd better make some kind of deal with Keats and his friends. They've already offered to buy the ranch."

"For once," he said, "it sounds like John is right."

Her face flushed with quick anger, and her gray eyes looked more like Aunt Kate's than ever. "I never expected to hear you say a thing like that."

He shrugged. "Listen, Marty. The country is changing. The days when Aunt Kate can rule the Box D and the rest of this part of the territory by ordering out a dozen riders with rifles are about past."

She stared at him. "I half believe you're lying to me, that you've been sent here by the railroad."

He started to protest, but she gave him no chance, turning quickly and opening the door. She didn't bother to close it, but moved rapidly down the stairs.

He almost went after her. Then he checked himself. That would never do. If Stivers ever realized that Marty Donovan had come to see him in his hotel room, the story would be all over Dondaro within an hour.

Slowly he turned back to his war bag. He had no real interest in the town, or the ranch, or the country. What happened to it was no affair of his. Let John and Bert Donovan worry about it. They would own the Box D when Kate finally died, if she ever did die. The old woman looked to be as husky as a tree. He thought that very possibly she might outlive them all as she had outlived her brothers.

He sat down on the edge of the bed, hardly knowing what to do with himself. He felt no real desire to talk to anyone in Dondaro, but the room was hot and, despite the open window, very close.

He rose finally and left the hotel. The wide street drowsed in the heat of the late afternoon. Half a dozen horses waited, scattered along the rails, their heads down, their tails whipping listlessly at the buzzing flies. Without definite purpose he moved along the unpeopled walk and paused before the Lone Star.

It was the biggest saloon that the town boasted, a long, low room with smoked ceiling and a lingering odor of stale beer. He turned in, knocking the batwing doors open with the heel of his hand, and stood for a full minute to let his eyes become accustomed to the darkness after the sun glare of the street.

Afterward, he moved ahead slowly. The saloon was nearly empty. A single apron stood behind the long counter, leaning forward upon it, his weight resting on his heavy forearms.

Ray Donovan glanced at the bartender and failed to recognize him. Then he looked toward the rear of the room where three loafers stood quietly, watching the five men who played at one of the poker tables.

There was no one in the crowd he knew. He had a drink at the bar and drifted over to stand silently himself, watching the fall of the cards. The Lone Star was like a hundred saloons he had known, scattered across the wide expanse of the West. In a country where there were ten men for every woman the saloon offered the natural meeting place, the public club where any man was welcome as long as he had money in his pocket.

The man at the far side of the table interested him. He was tall and well dressed, and he bore the unmistakable mark of the professional gambler.

Ray Donovan admired the long-fingered hands as they riffled the cards and dealt them easily. He watched closely for signs of trickery, but found none.

He had known many gamblers in the railroad camps. Some were experts with shaved decks, with second carding, with all the tricks of their highly skilled trade. Others were strangely honest, having a rigid code that they adhered to.

This man seemed to be honest, perhaps only because this game was small. At any rate, Donovan had the overpowering desire to find out. He could not explain the feeling to himself. He had never seen the gambler before, as far as he could recall, and would in all probability never see him again.

He pushed between two of the loafers and settled his big bulk into an empty seat.

"Open game?"

The five players glanced at him. Three were obviously cowboys by their dress, the fourth was a salesman of some kind, his cloth suit seeming a little out of place in this dusty room.

The gambler was the last to look up, and, when he did so, Ray Donovan received a shock. The man's eyes were a curious shade, a deep blue with a hint of red in them, almost a deep lavender. Yet it was not the color of the eyes that sharpened his attention but a glow of recognition in their depths, as if the man knew him and was surprised at seeing him there.

The game went on. He studied the gambler, trying to appear not to, trying to recall where he had seen the man and failing to do so.

At 6:00 the game broke up and he walked behind the gambler to the bar, pausing at his side. "A drink?"

The man turned, his long face an expressionless mask. Only his eyes seemed alive. The rest of him might have belonged to a corpse.

"Thank you, Mister Donovan."

Ray said nothing. The bartender served them and moved away. The gambler said: "You don't remember me, Mister Donovan?" His voice was soft with the slurring accent of the Old South.

"Should I?" Donovan was not looking at him directly, but watching him in the back-bar mirror.

"Butte," the gambler said, and smiled. "You ran the lot of us out of Butte. The name is Kandee. I don't suppose you ever saw me. I was just one of the crowd you cleaned out of town."

Donovan did not answer him. Donovan was thinking back over the years. He'd seen a lot of towns, a lot of people moved out. For the life of him he could not remember Kandee.

The gambler was studying him with those odd eyes. "So you'll come back here to stop them building their railroad?"

Donovan almost dropped his glass. "Say that again?"

The man smiled. When he smiled, it seemed to change his whole face, bringing it alive, adding a warmth that had not been there before. "You can't keep a secret in this country, Mister Tough Donovan. It's all over town that Kate brought you back here to stop them from building this railroad."

Donovan put the glass on the bar. Then he started to laugh. The gambler stared at him in surprise. "Perhaps," he murmured, "I've said something humorous without intending to?"

"It wasn't what you said," Donovan told him. "It's just that Kate thinks I've come back to build the railroad, and the men who are trying to build it seem to think I've come back to keep it from being built. I think that's funny."

Kandee's smile grew. "It is, if it's the truth."

Donovan looked at him, hard, but he realized that the man meant nothing by the remark. "It is the truth," he said soberly. "And all of them will know it tonight when I pull out on the evening stage."

The man at his side nodded. "It's probably good that you're leaving. They were getting ready to run you out of town."

Ray Donovan went utterly still. It was as if his muscles were frozen, as if he found it impossible to move. But his mind was not affected. He thought: *This is something. For years I've been the one to run others out of a town, and now, when I've come home for the first time in six years, this has to happen to me in my own home town.*

It was only a momentary paralysis. He seemed to awaken as if he was coming out of a coma and he thought he saw the shadow of mockery in the gambler's eyes.

"You don't like it," Kandee said in his soft voice. "You don't like the idea, do you, Mister Donovan?"

Ray shook his head. "I don't."

"But you will like it," said Kandee. "Just the way I liked it when you ordered us out of Butte. You had men at your back. All the tough construction crew from your railroad. But you have no one now, not unless you can bring in the Box D riders to help you."

Donovan shook his head. "They wouldn't help me. Kate would rather see me hanging to a tree than raise a hand to help me. I know her."

"Good bye," Kandee said. "It would be amusing to watch you stay and fight, but that's too much to expect." He turned then, and went away from Donovan. He passed through the batwing doors to the street beyond, a tall man, very thin but curiously graceful in his motions like a trained boxer, leaning forward a little as he walked, his weight perfectly balanced on the balls of his feet.

Donovan watched him out of sight, then turned back, intending to order another drink. Abruptly he changed his mind and left the saloon. The heat of the street had lessened as the sun dropped behind the western mountains and people were already stirring on the slatted sidewalks.

He recognized several he passed on his way toward the hotel, but he did not speak. He knew that he had changed in the years he had been away and he was not surprised that they failed to acknowledge him.

He came into the lobby and saw Wilbur Keats and Sam Friend waiting beside the desk, and knew instinctively that they awaited him. He did not know how he knew.

It was a kind of sixth sense that he had, a warning that rang clearly in his brain when danger pressed from any direction. It had saved his life more than once, and he acted on it now, walking directly toward them.

It was characteristic of Ray Donovan that he preferred to face a threat rather than avoid it. He approached Keats, studying the older man as he did so, trying to recall everything he had ever known about him. Keats had been in the country a dozen years. He had come in originally as a cattle buyer, and he had stayed, opening first a livery stable, and then a stage line. He was a heavy-set man, perhaps forty, with a fleshy sunburned face and sharp blue eyes that looked as cold and brittle as pieces of glass.

Sam Friend was a different type. Sam had come into the country with Keats, but behind him traveled a number of shadowy tales, of wildness below the border, of dead men in the brush. As far as Donovan knew, these things were stories only, for Sam had never caused trouble during his years in Dondaro. But the stories had persisted, and he regarded the man with renewed attention.

When he had gone away, he had been a boy, without experience, without the ability to judge people and their motives and their

94

hidden thoughts. That was all changed now. He examined Sam Friend in the light of his widened horizons and was almost shocked by what he saw.

There was a lurking devil in Sam Friend's gray-green eyes, in the reckless way he smiled, in his very way of standing, carelessly leaning against the desk. It was as if he held himself under control with difficulty, as if the inner violence that was the core of the man strained constantly for release, as if he wanted to fight for fighting's sake alone.

He had swung around when Donovan entered the lobby, and, as Donovan approached, he seemed to tighten like a spring being compressed under great pressure.

He smiled when Donovan halted before them, but the smile was wolfish and eager, as if he were only awaiting the opportunity to pit himself against the younger man. His voice was low and mocking as he said: "The great Ray Donovan. I've heard about you, boy. I've been wanting to meet you."

Keats knew the man at his side, and Keats apparently did not want trouble at the moment. His face got redder under its deep sunburn and he said, almost harshly: "Stop it, Sam."

Sam Friend's voice was elaborately casual.

"Why, what did I do, Wilbur? I was just carried away, somehow, meeting the great Mister Donovan . . . Tough Donovan who cleaned out all those construction camps."

He spoke to his employer, but he never took his mocking eyes from Donovan's face. He stood now, leaning away from the wall, his body bent a little forward, his thumbs hooked in the heavy cartridge belt that sagged about his waist, held down on the right side by the weight of the single gun.

The workings of Sam Friend's mind were obvious. Donovan had a reputation, and the challenge of that reputation was almost more than Friend could resist. He stood there, eager for Donovan to make his move, his hand ready to drop claw-like toward his holstered gun.

But Wilbur Keats grabbed his shoulder, pulling him half around, saying in sharp anger: "Not yet, Sam. Not yet."

Friend blew out his breath as if he had held it in his lungs too long, and said in a grumbling voice: "You're making a mistake, Wilbur, a great mistake." He turned away then, like a small boy who has been denied his greatest wish, and stalked out of the lobby.

Wilbur Keats tried to laugh, but it wasn't a great success. He sounded a little shaky, and Donovan glanced at him sharply. That laugh told him more about Keats than any words the man might have uttered.

Keats was nervous. Keats was not as sure of himself as he appeared, but when Keats spoke, he had mastered his uncertainty and sounded very confident. "I always liked you, Ray."

Donovan said nothing. He had learned something else. Keats was a liar. Keats had been barely conscious of his existence before he'd run away.

"I liked you," Keats said, and dampened his lips with the tip of his tongue. "And I don't want trouble with you. But this railroad is going to be built, and neither you nor your aunt Kate is going to stop us."

Donovan had the impulse to tell the man that Kate Donovan was no aunt of his, and that they could build fifty railroads as far as he was concerned. He almost said that he didn't care, that he was leaving on the night stage. But something stopped him.

Keats went on. "I understand you coming back here to help the old woman. You probably feel that you owe her a lot. But you can't do her any good. You can't stop us, any more than she has stopped us by shooting at our survey crews."

Ray still didn't answer. Keats mistook

silence for stubbornness and the redness of his face increased. "I'm not talking just to hear myself talk. I'm trying to avoid trouble. Sam Friend wanted to come in here and brace you. Sam used to be a bad boy before he came to work for me, and he fancies himself with a gun. It would be a feather in his cap to down you."

Donovan waited for more. Keats's anger seemed to increase with Donovan's continued silence. "I'm warning you, Ray. This town needs the railroad. This whole country needs the railroad. We're going to have it, and no old, bad-tempered woman is going to stop us. Oh, I know Kate Donovan will fight. I've known her for fifteen years. She thinks that she's a little tin god on wheels because the Box D is the biggest outfit in this end of the territory. She's always kept a tough crew, and she's always pushed everyone else around. But those days are over. If you throw in with Kate, every man, woman, and child in the country will be against you."

Donovan said, very low: "And what would you advise, Wilbur?"

"To get out," Keats said. "I don't know what the old lady promised you . . . probably a share in the ranch . . . but after the railroad runs through, there won't be enough of the ranch left to pay you. Go back to Denver. Go anywhere you like, but get out of here."

Had Wilbur Keats known more about Ray Donovan he might have taken warning from the way the skin seemed to tighten across the hinges of Donovan's jaw. But Wilbur Keats had never been too good a judge of men.

"And if I don't?" Donovan was still speaking in that quiet voice.

"Then I'll turn Sam Friend loose, and, if you do for Friend, there are still other men who will take care of you."

"Why not come yourself?" Donovan said. His voice was still soft but his blue eyes had darkened until they were almost black. "I'll show you what would happen if you did." He took a sudden step forward. His hands shot out, catching the lapels of the man's coat.

He jerked Wilbur Keats toward him. Keats's hand clawed for the gun at his side. Donovan slid his hold down to lock about the man's wrist. He pulled the gun free of the holster and pitched it clear across the lobby, hearing it strike the wall on the far side. Then he released his grip, stepped aside, and drove his fist squarely into Keats's face.

Wilbur Keats reeled backward until his shoulders struck the edge of the high desk. He seemed to hang there for a moment as if unable to regain his balance. Then, slowly, he slid down into a sitting position, his head lolling against the desk.

Donovan walked forward until he stood above Keats. "For your information," he said in a controlled voice, "I was planning on pulling out of here on the evening stage. I didn't come back here to block your railroad. I didn't have any idea of helping Kate. But I don't like being ordered out of any town, especially the town I consider home. I'm just chuckleheaded enough now to hang around and see what is actually going on. This country may need a railroad someday, but there isn't enough business through here right now to keep a railroad operating. There must be some answer to that and I'm going to wait around and find out what it is."

He left Keats there to think it over and climbed the stairs to his room.

After he closed the door and lighted the lamp, he crossed to the mirror and stood examining his face.

You're a fool, he thought. *A hammerheaded fool. This is not your business so why bother with it?*

Suddenly he grinned at himself. It was funny. First Kate, thinking he had come back to build the railroad, and then Keats, thinking that Kate had brought him back to stop it. He had told the truth to Marty. She'd believed him, but who else would ever believe him if he stayed? And he had made up his mind to stay. He would let no one run him out of this town.

In the hotel dining room, later, he noticed that half the people present were looking at him. Apparently the story had gotten abroad, and everyone in Dondaro thought that he was here to stop the building of the railroad.

He finished and strolled slowly out into the lobby, pausing to light a cigar and glance at the clock. 7:45. If he had not changed his mind, he would now be carrying his war bag down to the stage station.

He stepped out of the doorway and started across the wide gallery toward the steps. Then he stopped. Figures had come out of the shadows on each side of him. They rammed guns into his ribs, and a voice that he recognized as Sam Friend's said in his ear: "You're leaving, Tough Donovan, whether you like it or not." He felt Friend's hand come down and lift his gun from the holster. "Move on down the street," Friend said, and laughed as if he enjoyed this game. "Or have you the nerve to give us trouble? It would pleasure me to shoot you."

Donovan said around the cigar in the corner of his mouth: "I know it would, Sam, but it's a pleasure you won't have now or later."

"Maybe," Friend said, and managed to sound disappointed. "Maybe not. Hurry along, the stage is ready."

They walked along the street, three men abreast. To the casual passer-by they must have looked like three neighbors out for an evening walk, for Friend and his partner had returned their guns to their holsters, and each held Donovan loosely by an arm.

They crossed the wide street, angling through the deep dust and coming up behind the stage. Another man followed them and passed them to throw Donovan's war bag into the boot. This, he realized, was no accident. His leaving had been carefully planned. Within him was a cold, calm, calculating anger. He did not want to leave but he saw no way out of it.

"Get in," Friend said, and motioned to the stage.

Donovan looked around. He saw a man standing in the shadows by the building, and recognized him as the gambler, Kandee.

Abruptly, even before Kandee spoke, he knew that the gambler meant to take a hand in the game.

"A minute," Kandee said. He stepped away from the building and a small gun appeared in his hand.

Sam Friend and his partner froze with surprise. Ray Donovan laughed. The sound came out of him like a gust of air, rounded and full-blown.

"It looks," he said, "as if the game is not played yet." He pivoted neatly on the ball of his left foot and drove his fist into Sam Friend's face.

III

Sam Friend's body slammed back against the high wheel of the stagecoach, but he didn't go down. He charged directly at Donovan, drawing his gun, taking a vicious, full-armed, barrel-whipping swing at Donovan's head.

Ray ducked. The gun thumped down across the point of his left shoulder, almost paralyzing the arm.

Friend brought the gun up quickly for a second blow, but Ray reached out with his right hand and caught the man's wrist. Swinging half around, he used Friend's extended arm as a lever to throw the man directly over his head.

Sam Friend crashed down in the dust of the street with enough force to drive the wind out of him. For an instant he lay too stunned to move, and in that instant Donovan wrenched the gun from his grasp. Donovan spun around just as Friend's partner charged, ignoring the threat of the silent gambler's gun.

Donovan dropped his shoulder and caught the rush, taking contact precisely in the middle of the man's waist. His arms locked about the back of the man's knees and he straightened with the man hung across his shoulder like a sack of flour.

He spun around and threw the man from him, hearing his head crack against the steel tire of the stage wheel, seeing him drop senselessly to the street.

But he had no time to think. Sam Friend was already on his knees, clambering upward, and the man who had been carrying Donovan's war bag was clawing for his gun.

Donovan caught Friend by his shirt front, jerked him upright. He threw Friend into the second man, and they went down together. He stooped and recovered Friend's gun, then stood with it in his hand, breathing heavily, watching them untangle themselves and rise slowly, both dazed.

From the side he heard Kandee's mocking tones, saying without feeling: "You do play rough, friend Donovan. You do for a fact."

Donovan paid no attention. He waited until Friend was upright, then said evenly: "You're through, Sam. You and these two. If I find you in town after the stage pulls out, I'll kill you."

He didn't wait for their answers. He collected his own gun and the two from the other men, tossed the war bag on his shoulder, then turned to Kandee. "Come along. I want to talk to you."

The gambler dropped his own gun into its hide-out holster and walked along silently at Donovan's side. They climbed the stairs to Donovan's room and Donovan lighted the lamp on the dresser. Kandee seated himself on the bed and only then did Donovan speak.

"What made you do it?" he said.

Kandee arched his brows. The gesture made his long face seem longer than it really was and a humorous quirk tugged at the corner of his thin mouth. "You're a hard man, Donovan. Most people would be thanking me for pulling them out of a hole instead of questioning my motives."

"Most people wouldn't have managed to stay alive in some of the spots that I've seen," Donovan told him. "The reason I'm here tonight is because I'm usually careful."

"You weren't tonight."

"No," the big man admitted. "I wasn't tonight. I figured the roughing up I gave Keats would keep them quiet for a while. It's a mistake I won't make again."

"You've already made one. You took their guns, but you should have stayed and watched Sam Friend get on that stage. They can always borrow more guns."

"And what good would that have done? They could get off the stage at the edge of town."

"That they could. Sam Friend will be gunning for you. I know him and I know his type. A man like you, with your reputation, is a challenge he can't resist. If he doesn't come for you tonight, he will tomorrow or the next day, or the day after that. I would never sleep easy if I knew a man like Friend was on my trail."

"What are you suggesting?"

The gambler looked at him speculatively. "I'd suggest that you run. It seemed from what you said this afternoon that you intended to leave town."

"I've changed my mind."

"Why?"

Donovan thought about that for one full, silent minute. "Maybe it's because I don't like being run out of my home town," he said slowly. "Or maybe it's because I'm curious to know what fool would build a railroad into this country. Or maybe I just changed my mind for no reason at all."

Kandee shook his head. "It won't wash, Donovan."

"What won't wash?"

"Your changing your mind for no reason at all. I'll venture to say that never in your life have you ever changed your mind without a reason. It wouldn't be Bert, now, would it?"

Donovan looked startled. "Bert? You mean Bert Donovan? Why should Bert make me stay here?"

"You brought him home, didn't you? You might want to stay and protect his rights."

"I don't get what you're talking about." Donovan's tone was stiff. "I don't understand you at all. You seem to know a lot about my business and a lot about the Donovans."

Kandee's smile was a little wolfish. "A man in my profession makes it a practice to know all he can about the people from whom he draws his living. Bert Donovan

107

was one of my main sources of income before he went away. I'm glad to see that he's back, and I hate to see him lose his share in the ranch, unless he loses it to me."

Donovan stared at the gambler. He simply could not make Kandee out. He could never tell when the man was being serious and when he was being sarcastic. He said, half angrily: "Stop playing games with me. You still haven't bothered to tell me why you troubled to take Sam Friend and his two pards off my back. I've never been a customer of your poker game, and, if I ever am, I'll probably beat you."

Kandee's teeth were very white and they showed now in a quick smile. "The thing I could like about you, Donovan, is your deep pride. You can't beat me playing cards. In fact, I doubt if you could beat me with a gun. But I'm not fool enough to find out. I'll tell you frankly why I took your part tonight. I figured you'd come back here to help Marty Donovan. I still figure that's the reason . . . and as long as you are on the side of the little lady I'll back your play. Believe me, she needs help, and needs it badly. More than I can give her alone." He rose as he spoke and moved toward the door.

Donovan's throat went dry. He cleared it

noisily. "What's Marty Donovan to you, Kandee?"

The gambler pulled open the door before he answered. "Why, nothing," he said, "except a flower growing in a barren land. Sometimes a man is hungry for water. Sometimes for whiskey. And sometimes for beauty. There's very little beauty in the world, Donovan, very little." He stepped out into the hall, shutting the door quietly behind him.

Donovan stared at the closed panel. His impulse was to follow Kandee, to grasp him by the shirt front where the ruffles were held together by the diamond pin, to shake him until he got the truth out of him. Marty and a gambler — it didn't make sense. None of this made any sense.

He turned slowly from the door, relaxing as he sat down on the bed. He wanted to think, to think carefully. There was too much here that he did not understand.

He sat there for perhaps twenty minutes. He did not hear the first light tap on the door. The second, louder, roused him from his deep study. He stiffened, wondering who it was.

Certainly it was no friend. He had no friend in Dondaro. He rose, shifting the gun in his holster to make certain it was free.

Then he called: "Come in!"

Marty Donovan slipped into the room, closing the door quickly behind her as if she were afraid that someone might have seen her entrance. Then he saw the storm in her gray eyes.

"Why, Marty, what . . . ?"

"Don't talk to me." Her slender body was stiff with fury. "I never expected you to lie to me."

He was taken completely unaware. "Lie to you?"

"You said you didn't come here to help build this railroad. You said you were leaving on the evening stage. And I believed you. I even rode in to where the ranch road connects with the highway and stopped the stage. I wanted to say good bye. I wanted to thank you for bringing Bert home. And then the driver told me that you weren't on board."

Donovan smiled faintly. He took a step forward and caught her shoulders between his two hands. "Calm down, Marty. Did he tell you about the fight I had with Keats's men? Did you see Sam Friend on the stage?"

"I did not. It was empty, and don't try to change the subject." She had made no effort to free herself, but now she brought down the sharp heel of her right boot on his left instep. He let out an involuntary yell and jumped back.

"Why, you little devil . . . !"

"And keep your hands off me. The next time I'll use a gun."

She wasn't fooling. There was a lot of Kate Donovan in this tall niece. She might be very young, but there was a set to her chin and to the cant of her mouth that warned him that, once embarked on a course, she would not change.

He said softly: "I believe you would at that. Listen, Marty. What makes you think that I'd lie to you?"

"Because you hate Aunt Kate. Because you'd go a long way out of your path to get even with her."

He said reflectively: "You're right. I do hate her, and, when I left here six years ago, I'd have gone very far out of my way to do her a disservice. But that's past."

"I don't believe you."

He gazed down at her, helpless.

"And I'll tell you something else. If I catch you trying in any way to force the railroad across the ranch, I'll shoot you." She whirled and headed for the door.

"Wait a minute."

She didn't wait. She flung the door open

and slipped into the hall. She slammed the door in his face.

By the time he had jerked it open, she was already at the head of the stairs. He called her name and strode after her, but she went down the steps lightly, like a bird in flight, and darted across the lobby. Before he could reach the lower level, she slammed the outer door and disappeared onto the gallery.

A voice called his name. Swinging about, he found Kandee in the shadowed corner of the long room. "Donovan, wait!"

For an instant Donovan's soul was black with murder. "Kandee," he said slowly and distinctly, "the next time you interfere in my affairs, I'll kill you."

Kandee did not seem to be impressed. In fact, Donovan had never met anyone who seemed less impressed by passing events than was the tall gambler.

"I judge," Kandee said, "that Miss Donovan did not like the idea of your remaining in this town."

"She's not the only one," Donovan said shortly. "Sam Friend and his men didn't ride the stage out of town."

Kandee said: "I know. They're waiting for you, down beyond the livery stable. I told you to put them on the stage."

Donovan looked up the dark street. The

sidewalks held their share of evening traffic; the horses along the rails stomped restlessly. It was as peaceful a scene as a man could imagine, yet, just beyond the corner, death waited for Tough Donovan to appear.

IV

Martha Donovan had ridden this street a hundred times in her eighteen years. Dondaro was her home, and, as the niece of Kate Donovan, she had been treated always by the shopkeepers and merchants with extreme courtesy.

In a sense Dondaro had always been a Box D town. The ranch was the biggest payroll in the county, and Kate Donovan had always taken an active interest in local politics.

Now for some reason that she could not explain Marty Donovan had a sense of foreboding as she moved along the wide street toward where she had tethered her horse at the side of the livery corral.

But she reached the horse without incident, and was about to step into the saddle when she saw the three men in the shadows ahead of her.

She stopped, standing perfectly quiet, listening. None of them had seen her, and this grouping of three men in the darkness would not ordinarily have caught her notice. But coupled with her feeling of impending danger, she found their fugitive attitude alarming.

For five minutes they failed to move, and she was about to ride out when something down the street attracted their attention. Glancing around, she saw that Donovan had come from the hotel and was standing clearly outlined in the broad yellow band of light from the big front window.

She looked back at the men. They were on the sidewalk while she stood in the deep dusk of the street, half hidden between her horse and the one tied next to it.

They were moving now, the three of them, all carrying their guns in their hands, and she drew a quick breath as she realized that they were staking Donovan.

Her rifle was in the boot under her stirrup flap. She pulled it free without pausing to think, and levered a shell into the chamber.

She had been handling guns since she had been able to hold one to her shoulder, and she had been raised in this far land where everything was violence. It neither appalled nor frightened her that she might kill a man. She thought no more about it than she would have thought about blowing the head from a coiled rattler.

They were ahead of her now, almost half a block away, and they separated, one of them crossing to the opposite sidewalk, one staying on her side of the street, while Sam Friend took the center of the roadway.

It was obvious that they meant to brace Donovan from three angles, and the girl's mouth tightened. No one man, not even if he were Ray Donovan, could hope to face fire from three directions at once. Marty Donovan changed her plan.

She quickly loosened the rein that held her horse at the rail and swung lightly up into the saddle. A moment later she came charging down the street like a cyclone, her hair loose and unrestrained by her hat that now hung at her back by the chin strap, riding out behind her like a plume.

She swept past Sam Friend and his men and tore directly toward the hotel, almost running Donovan down as she slid the startled horse to a quick stop.

"Ray. They're coming, three of them." She kicked her foot free from the stirrup on his side. "Come on."

Ray Donovan's life had been one of split-second decisions. He didn't hesitate. He caught the horn with one hand, kicked into the vacant stirrup, and a moment later was behind her on the horse.

The startled animal went out of Dondaro at a frightened run as if he carried a feather upon his back instead of a double load.

Behind them Sam Friend sent up a high, angry cry through the night, and snapped a shot at the fleeing horse, only to have Wilbur Keats call to him angrily from the doorway of one of the darkened stores.

"Take it easy, you fool! If you hit that girl, we'll all wind up at the end of a rope."

Friend crossed toward him, saying in a savage undertone: "You told us she was sore at him."

"She is. At least that's what the boss said."

"It looked like it," Friend said. He was staring down the empty street through which Donovan and Marty had passed only a few moments before. Then he thought of something else.

"Where's that gambler, Kandee, fit into all this?"

"He doesn't," Keats said. "Not that I know of, he doesn't."

"He butted in when we were putting Donovan on the stage."

Keats was quiet, thinking. "Maybe he just didn't like the idea of three men against one."

"It's too bad what he likes." Friend swore

under his breath. He was feeling angry, and cheated, and, since Ray Donovan was for the moment apparently beyond reach, he turned his attention to Kandee.

"I never liked him. He's a little too slick with his cards for my taste, and he acts like he was better than any man on earth. I'm going to find him."

But Sam Friend did not find the gambler that night. Whatever else Kandee was, he was not stupid, and, having witnessed Donovan's fleeing the town on the back of the girl's horse, he sought his own hiding place, cutting down Marcus Alley, behind the Great Dipper Saloon, and turning into the house that Peggy Squires operated.

Peggy was not glad to see him. She was a big-boned woman who had once been handsome but whose looks had faded, leaving her haggard and washed out, her dyed hair looking more like a wig than something that grew upon her head.

"You in trouble again." She said it bluntly the instant Kandee stepped into the parlor.

There were three girls in the room, resembling so many expressionless dolls with their painted faces and thin dresses under which they wore nothing at all.

His eyes swept the line of girls and settled on Peggy. "Is that the way you greet all your guests, my dear? If it is, I should wonder how you continue in your profession."

Her mouth was hard. "Look, Kandee. You never come here unless you're in trouble. As far as I know, you couldn't come here for any other reason."

He laughed then, and the laughter brought on a fit of coughing. He drew a white handkerchief from the sleeve of his carefully tailored coat and dabbed at his lips with the bit of laced linen. A spot of red showed upon the handkerchief. He stared at it a moment, and then hastily put it out of sight.

As soon as the coughing started, Peggy Squires's whole manner changed. She took his arm and with a curious softness led him back through a connecting door into her own private sitting room, shutting the door and saying angrily as she put him into a big chair: "You fool, when will you learn to take care of yourself? What do you want to do . . . die in my parlor and give my business a bad name?"

He used the handkerchief again to wipe his lips and humor lighted his overly bright eyes. "Peggy, Peggy, there's no one like you. We're outcasts, you and I, and yet we can still laugh at life. As long as people can laugh, they're all right. Nothing very serious can happen to them."

He was silent a moment, striving to keep down his cough. Then, succeeding, he added: "Better tell the girls that if anyone comes asking, I'm not here."

She said: "Don't worry. They all know better than to tell anything to anyone. Who's thirsting for your blood now, Kandee?"

"Sam Friend and some more of Keats's men."

She swore softly under her breath. "You are a fool. Why did you have to run up against Friend? The man's a killer. He's crazy. As well hand a mad dog a fresh set of teeth as to give him a full-loaded gun. They both will start charging around, looking for someone to use them on."

Kandee smiled.

Instead Peggy shivered. "You think it's funny," she said. "Well, I don't. I know men. Men are my business and how to control them and please them is my stock in trade. But I want no part of Sam Friend. What made you tangle with him?"

"He and his pals tried to load Ray Donovan on the stage."

Her dark eyes got smoky. She didn't ask who Donovan was. She tried to know who everyone in the country was and who they tied in with. Her ability to keep operating depended on her ability to judge correctly the forces that controlled this town.

"And why did you have to take Tough Donovan's part?"

"Because it pleased me," said Kandee. "Because a man who is dying finds little interest in life outside of amusement. Donovan amuses me. He's so big and strong, so quick and tough. He's everything that I'm not and never will be again."

"Don't talk like that."

"The truth," he said, and looked at her with eyes that held their hint of fever. "The truth, Peggy. No man ever suffered from knowing the truth and facing it."

She said flatly: "I don't understand you. I never have and I guess I never will. I thought first that, when you started coming here, you came to hide. But it's not that. You aren't afraid of anything."

"No," he said. "I'm not afraid, not in the way you mean. I could go out and face Sam Friend and perhaps kill him. And if I didn't, if he killed me, it wouldn't really matter because it would only hasten the inevitable by a little while. But if that occurred, I'd never know what happened to Donovan."

She was still suspicious. "What's this Ray Donovan to you?"

"A symbol," he told her, smiling. "He's no friend. He ran me out of one of his railroad camps once, along with the other gamblers, the grafters, and the girls. He is what I might have been if circumstances had been different. In watching him, I am in fact watching the man I might have been. It's a privilege that is granted to few people."

She said, half sulkily: "You're a funny one. I don't know why I put up with you."

"Because I'm like a homeless dog." His smile was still in place. "You've got a kind heart, Peggy."

"You'd find very few people in this town to agree with you." Her tone was sharp as if she resented being caught in doing a kindness to anyone. "But my heart isn't big enough to cover Ray Donovan. He came back here to stop this new railroad, and I want the road. It will make this town, and help my business, and. . . ."

"There isn't going to be any railroad," Kandee told her.

"You mean because Donovan will stop it?"

"I mean because the men who applied for the charter never intended to build it in the first place."

"I don't believe that. I don't believe you know what you're talking about."

He shrugged.

She was still suspicious. "Don't try to be mysterious with me, Kandee. I'm staking a lot on this railroad. I'm having the house remodeled and enlarged."

"Don't."

"But why should they start to build a railroad, or say they were going to build a railroad, when they didn't intend to do it?"

"Because," he told her, "the human mind is sometimes more crooked than a cattle trail. Who has most of the money in this part of the country?"

"The Donovans."

"Kate Donovan," he corrected her. "The old woman owns the ranch, and the stock, and the bank here in town, and about everything else that's worth having in this part of the world."

"That's why I can't understand her not wanting the railroad to come in."

"That's why she doesn't want it to come in," he explained. "You don't know much about how railroads are built and financed, do you, Peggy? Well, the government back in Washington is interested in seeing the West opened up. On some of the early roads they paid the builders a cash subsidy, so much for every mile of track that was laid. On other roads, where the right of way crossed government land, they gave the railroad company every alternate section so that the company could sell the land to settlers and build up business along its tracks."

"I don't see what that has to do with Kate Donovan."

"Don't you? Well, I'll tell you. The Box D runs over thirty thousand head of cattle. They graze over nearly five million acres. It's one of the biggest ranches left anywhere in the country that's still privately owned, and with all these cattle, the only deeded land they control is a section here and there where there's water. The rest of the graze is on government land. Now suppose a railroad comes down through the pass to the north and heads for Dondaro. They'll run catty-corner across the full length of the ranch, and they'll own a strip of staggered sections that will cut the Box D directly in two."

She was staring at him.

"What would you do if you were Kate Donovan?"

"Fight."

"Sure. And if it looks as if you are going to lose the fight?"

"Pay off."

"That," he told her, "is exactly what the men behind this railroad scheme are counting on. They expect to have Kate pay them off and pay them off big."

"Who are they?" He merely smiled at her

and the suspicion was back in her eyes. "You?"

He laughed then. "What would a dying man want with thirty thousand head of cattle or a million acres of ground? No, Peggy. Don't get strange ideas in your head. I'm not the one behind this."

"It can't be Wilbur Keats." She was speaking to herself. "He isn't smart enough."

"No," Kandee agreed. "Keats isn't smart enough. He's just the front man, the hired help, the one who stands up to be shot at. But don't try to guess, Peggy. It's safer if you don't know. The man who dreamed up this little plan is as ruthless as they come. He wants the ranch, and he'll stop at nothing including murder to get it."

She squinted at him. "You seem to know a great deal about this, and about the Donovans. How did you find out so much about this railroad scheme?"

His smile was thin. "Sam Friend misjudged me. Sam thought anyone would do anything for money. Sam got drunk one night. Or should I say, I helped him get drunk one night? Anyway, he bragged about the deal. And then he offered me ten thousand in gold to get Bert Donovan into a card game, and then into an argument over the cards, and then to kill him."

She was horrified. "Kill Bert deliberately?"

He nodded.

"But why should they do that? What would they gain? Were they going to have John killed, too?"

He merely shrugged.

"But what did you do?"

He said: "I sent word to Bert to get out of the country for a while. He disappeared and he didn't come back until today."

She made a clucking noise. "And tonight you stood up against Sam and his friends. They will kill you as soon as they can."

"Probably."

"Why do you tell me this?"

He hesitated. He had meant to tell Ray Donovan the whole story, but he didn't quite trust Ray, not yet. And he had needed to talk to someone. This thing was eating at him inside. He had been in love with Marty Donovan from the first moment he saw her. He had been new to town then, two years ago, and he had stood on the sidewalk and watched her ride by, not knowing who she was, not caring, knowing even then that he had been marked by death, and that she was not for him.

But he loved her. He clung to the thought as a drowning man will cling to a straw. It had kept him alive, giving him a purpose he would not otherwise have had.

In these years he had spoken to her no more than four or five times — spoken as a stranger does, merely passing the time of day. Yet he watched her, and watched over her, and made it his practice to know what happened to the Donovans because it affected her. He cared nothing for the rest of the family, but he knew that sooner or later he might be called upon to kill for her, and he knew he would be ready.

This was something he could not discuss with Peggy, with anyone. This was something he kept carefully locked in his slender chest, his secret, the only thing that made the world bearable for him.

"I just wanted to talk," he said to Peggy. "Once in a while a man simply has to talk."

V

Marty Donovan let her horse run across the wooden bridge that spanned the Río Bravo and out along the twisting road that meandered ten miles to the Box D headquarters. When they had covered perhaps half a mile, Ray told her to pull up and she brought the horse to a stop.

"This should be far enough," he said. "Friend doesn't seem to be following."

He swung to the ground, but she held her place in the saddle, looking down at him. "What are you going to do now?"

He shrugged. "Go back to the hotel, I suppose."

She said: "They'll be waiting for you. They'll have you in another corner. You can't fight them all alone."

He grinned up at her. "Half an hour ago you were going to shoot me yourself."

Her face gained color in the moonlight and she said sharply: "Ray, if you're here to help the railroad, why were Sam Friend and his men waiting for you?"

"I told you I wasn't."

"Then why did you stay in town?"

He wanted to tell her again that he did not like being run out of any place, then he stopped, saying instead: "I've already tried to make you understand and you didn't believe me."

Impulsively she put out a small hand to rest on his shoulder. "I don't know what's the matter with me, Ray. It's just that everything has become so strange in the last few months, until I don't trust anyone, even myself."

He stared up at her. The moon was full and its soft light made her seem only the more attractive. This was the child he had taught to ride, who had tagged his footsteps all during their growing years. He had loved her then, but the feeling was little akin to the one that was shaking him now.

He said, steadying his voice with an effort: "What's bothering you . . . this projected railroad?"

She raised a hand to shove her hat back off her small head so that the downdraft of the evening wind stirred her hair. "It isn't only that. Things at the ranch have changed since you went away. Or maybe they haven't changed so much, but I notice them more than I did when I was younger. We Donovans live in a pool of hate."

"Because of Aunt Kate?"

She moved her hand in a little sweeping gesture. "Not only Kate, though you know how she is, how she always has been. As she gets older, she's harder to live with. She now has the idea that she's going to die, and that all of us . . . John, Bert, and I . . . are just sitting there, watching like a bunch of vultures until she's gone.

"It isn't true of course. She's sixty-five, but she's still strong as a horse and unless she has an accident she'll live another twenty years. But she hates John. She lets him run the ranch, yet she picks on him all the time. He can't make a decision or sign a check without her OK. She picks on Bert, although she favors him above John and John knows it. And she picks on me for the things that Bert does. She seems to feel they're my fault, that I could make him behave if I chose."

Her voice as she said this last had flattened and gained a note of weariness. "What makes people the way they are? There never was a more likable person in the world than Bert when he isn't drinking, and I think half his drinking and gambling is nothing but rebellion against Aunt Kate. She orders him around constantly. She even tries to tell him what he can and can't eat."

Ray smiled in spite of himself.

"I don't feel at home any more. A lot of the old crew has gone . . . I don't think they liked taking John's orders . . . and the new men aren't the same."

"Patches still there?" Patches had been foreman when Ray was a boy, a small, bandy-legged man with leathery cheeks and sharp, all-seeing eyes.

"He's pretty well retired," Marty said. "He got thrown from a horse last year and he's badly broken up. He stays at one of the northern camps and seldom comes in to the home ranch."

Donovan wondered why he was bothering

to ask these questions. He kept telling himself that the ranch and family meant nothing to him. But the girl did count.

She said suddenly: "Come to the ranch with me tonight. It isn't safe for you to go back to town alone."

His smile was thin. "And if Kate Donovan had anything to do with it, it wouldn't be very safe for me at the ranch."

"You know that isn't the truth. Kate was sorry for the way she acted almost as soon as you ran away, and she was sorry today after you'd left."

His smile became a little mocking. "Marty, Marty, you're just trying to make me feel better."

She said sharply: "It isn't that. We Donovans have a nasty habit of saying things we don't mean. In her way Kate's been proud of you. She read in the papers about how you cleaned out the railroad camps."

"And now she believes I came here to help build this road through her ranch."

"I don't think she actually believes that."

"You did."

She said slowly: "Don't fight me, Ray. I was shocked when I stopped the stagecoach and didn't find you on it. I was afraid something had happened to you. Then when I found you safe at your hotel, I was mad at myself for being worried, and I didn't know what to believe. Please help me."

"How?"

"Come back to the ranch and talk to Aunt Kate. She was angry this morning because Bert hadn't come home by himself, but in effect had been dragged home by you. She feels guilty for the way she treated you six years ago, and she hates the thought of being under obligation to you."

"It's no good," he told her. "I don't belong at the Box D."

"You do," she said. "Come out there tonight, if for no other reason than because I ask you."

It was hard for him to refuse Marty Donovan. No, he couldn't refuse.

"All right," he said. "But don't be disappointed if it doesn't work out the way you expect it to."

"I expect nothing," she said. "I've learned to expect nothing and hope for the best. I only hope that Aunt Kate will not act the fool, and that you will be reasonably courteous because I ask you to."

Her hope was not borne out. They came into the Box D yard to find the lights still burning in the living room of the big house. They went up the walk together, reaching the porch just as the door was pulled open.

Kate Donovan stepped into the entrance, staring out.

"Marty, is that you? Where have you been?"

They were in the shadow cast by the porch and she could not see them plainly.

The girl answered softly: "I've been to town."

"And what were you doing in town?" The voice, more like a man's than a woman's, was harsh and accusing. "I've told you not to ride alone at night."

"I wasn't alone," Marty told her. "I went in to see Ray. He came back with me."

The old woman was perfectly quiet, holding herself erect. She looked rigid, massive, immovable. "And what does Ray want here?"

"To talk with you." A pleading note had crept into Martha Donovan's voice. "Please, Aunt Kate, talk to him."

"I have nothing to say."

Marty's fingers closed over Ray's arm with surprising strength. She squeezed as if warning him not to speak yet.

"But he has something to say to you."

"Probably hopes to talk me into not opposing that railroad. Well, he can save his breath."

"He has nothing to do with the railroad."

"Then why is he here?"

"He met Bert in Denver and decided to come home with him. After all, Aunt Kate, this is his home, about the only home he's ever known." She was openly pleading now, her voice shaking with intensity. "You feed any chance rider who comes through here and never give it a second thought. Surely you have at least one kind word for a man who has always considered himself your nephew."

For a moment the old woman gave no sign that she had heard, and it seemed to Marty, watching her aunt's rock-like figure, that she had failed. Then Kate Donovan said grudgingly: "All right, both of you come in."

They crossed the porch and entered the long room in silence. Ray Donovan had expected to find Kate alone. She wasn't. Both Bert and John Donovan sat at the long table.

Bert raised one hand mockingly: "My savior. Welcome to the battlefield, Ray."

John merely nodded. He was a dry man, older than his brother in both age and manner. There was no humor in John Donovan. He watched the world with deep and studied seriousness.

Kate ignored her two nephews, giving her

full attention to the newcomer. For his part Ray glanced quickly around the big room, noting how little it was changed. This had been his home, and each furred rug, each piece of furniture had its memories. Once he had felt that he belonged here, that he would spend the rest of his life on the huge ranch. Then, after his break with Kate, he had never thought to enter this room again.

She was watching him, her gray eyes as unreadable as slate, and as hard. "I hope you like what you see." Her tone was dry with unfriendliness. "I never expected you to come back here."

Marty said with quick fierceness: "He wouldn't have come tonight if I hadn't made him."

Her aunt did not appear to hear the words. "What did you come for?" Her tone was accusing and it brought Ray Donovan's quick anger up to meet hers.

"I didn't come to see you," he said. "All the time I was growing up, I didn't love you. You aren't the kind of person who invokes much love, Aunt Kate."

She showed neither anger nor amusement.

"But I respected you," he said, "and I was grateful for what you did for me. I'm still grateful, but I ceased to respect you the day you jumped me after my fight with John, telling me that I had no name, and that I didn't belong here without ever giving me the chance to explain my side of the fight."

As he spoke, his eyes flicked for an instant to John Donovan's face. It was expressionless. The eyes watched Ray without any change, without feeling.

"You're feeling sorry for yourself," Kate said.

"I did feel sorry for myself," he admitted. "I was a kid then. I'd never been called upon to face anything like that and I didn't know how. But I learned. I learned quickly. I was thrown with men who did not give a damn whether my name was Donovan, or Smith, or whether I ever had a name. All that interested them was what I could do and how well I could do it."

"So you became a hired bully." There was a flick of contempt in the old woman's tone. "Tough Donovan. Do you feel tough, Ray? How many notches have you filed in your gun handle?"

He knew that she was deliberately trying to anger him further, and he resolved not to let her words disturb him. "I did what I had to do," he said. "You can't build a railroad when every gambler and loose woman in the West is preying on the workers."

"The railroad," she said. "So now you

come here to force a railroad across my land, the land that raised you, that paid for your food and clothes." She was working herself up into one of her famous rages, but he stopped her with a sentence.

"I don't think that any of us will live to see a railroad run into Dondaro."

She opened her mouth once, like a fish out of water and gasping, then she closed it slowly. Ray Donovan was conscious that both Bert and John were watching him with grave attention.

"You're a fool." Kate Donovan had recovered her breath. "The charter has been granted for every other section of land, as soon as the right of way is graded and preliminary survey crews have strung their stakes clear across the ranch. I ought to know. I ran them off and I had the stakes pulled up."

Ray Donovan turned toward the east wall. There, covering a third of the space, hung a huge map of the territory. On it, in red, was marked the seemingly endless range of the Box D, an irregular block of color that took in a good half of five mountain counties.

"Here," he said, standing before the map. "If you're going to build into Dondaro from the north, your only connection would be with the D and RG." His finger traced down the possible route. "I've ridden those hills, all of them, and anyone who thinks he can build a railroad through them knows nothing about the cost of putting in a road. It would be cheaper to put in rails and sleepers of solid gold than it would to grade that right of way."

No one said anything. For once in her life Kate Donovan was stilled.

"And where would you go from Dondaro?" His finger moved on, indicating the rugged country to the south. "Here, to connect with the Atlantic and Pacific? Why? There's no country in between to support a road. There isn't enough passenger traffic to run one train a month, and the only freight would be cows from this ranch and the smaller outfits."

Kate Donovan moistened her lips. "Then why are they building it?"

"They aren't, yet." He faced around and came slowly back to the table. "All I've heard mentioned is a survey party and some stakes. What does a survey party amount to? A few men and a grub wagon and a transit. As for stakes, you can cut a million of them in the hills."

"But. . . ."

"I've written to three men I know, men who would be able to give me the answers.

If a new road is to be built through here, they'll know all about it . . . who's behind it, how much money they have, what chance they have of financing their bonds in the East, whether any contracts have been let for grading, whether any rails and rolling stock have been ordered."

"But we know that Wilbur Keats is behind it," Kate Donovan cut in.

Ray Donovan smiled for the first time since entering the house. "Who is Keats? A saloonkeeper, a gambling game owner, a minor cattle buyer, a small stage-line operator. That kind of man doesn't build railroads."

John Donovan spoke for the first time. "You always did jump at things, Ray, even when you were a boy." There was reproof in the tone and no tolerance. It was this intolerance in John Donovan that had caused the fight long ago, the fight that led to Ray's running away. "But it's understandable," John continued as they all turned to look at him. "You have nothing at stake, no part of the Box D. With us it's different. Everything the family owns is tied up in this ranch. The break in beef prices almost ruined us three years ago. We had to sell most of the bank stock, and we borrowed heavily from some of the commission men in Kansas City. We simply can't afford to have trouble now."

"And what do you propose to do about it?"

"That," said John deliberately, "is none of your business."

It came to Ray suddenly that John Donovan did not want him in this room, did not want him on the ranch, or for that matter in this part of the country.

They had never pretended to like each other, even when they were boys, and it might merely be this old feeling that was driving John to insult him, to anger him so much that he would leave as he had left once before.

He glanced quickly toward Marty and found that her eyes were on him, appealing to him to hold his temper, to help her somehow. He looked at Bert. There was a humorous quirk to Bert's wide mouth. Bert was amused by this scene as Bert was amused by a great deal of life. He liked Bert, and his feeling for Marty was much stronger, and in the final analysis this was their ranch. It would be once Kate's hold failed. Being in the majority, it would be their ranch to hold or to lose, not John's, and he meant suddenly to see that they held it.

He turned to Kate. "In the old days you were always short of riders. Are you still hiring?"

She blinked at him, not quite comprehending what was in his mind. "We're always short-handed." Her voice was curt.

"Then I'm looking for a job." He kept his face perfectly straight as he said it. "I was trained under the smartest ranch owner I've ever known, a woman named Donovan."

She got what he meant then, but she did not believe it. "We only pay forty and found," she said. "Furnish your own saddle."

"He can have one of mine." It was Bert, still looking sleepily amused.

"He can have his own!" It was Marty, relief and gratitude shining deeply in her eyes. "I've kept it ever since he sold it in Dondaro, six years ago. I bought it back."

John Donovan said angrily: "What are you up to now, Ray? You can make four hundred a month with any railroad in the country. I wouldn't hire you if you were the last man on earth."

Kate Donovan said surprisingly: "I'm still running the ranch, John. Marty, get that saddle. Bert, take him over to the bunkhouse."

For a moment it looked as if John Donovan would jump to his feet and oppose his aunt, then he slumped slackly back into his chair as if he realized that the argument was hopeless.

Marty let out a little quick laugh. She almost ran from the room.

Bert cocked an eyebrow at his aunt, then without comment shambled to his feet and motioned Ray toward the door. When they had gone, John said savagely: "Why'd you do that? You know there's something behind this. I'll give you any odds that he's here as a spy. Tough Donovan hasn't worked for forty a month in years."

His aunt's eyes were on the door through which Bert and their newest hand had disappeared. "I know it," she said, "and I don't trust him any more than you do. But if I have him on the ranch, I can watch him. I can order him where I want him to go, and I might even arrange that something would happen to him, something I'm pretty certain he wouldn't like."

John Donovan gaped at her. Then suddenly he smiled. It was the first smile he had permitted himself in several days.

VI

The bunkhouse at the Box D was big and made of logs. It was one of the original buildings that old man Donovan had raised when he drove his herd of Texas-bred cattle across the sandy wastes of the south and chose to settle on this rising shoulder of the green hills.

Ray Donovan followed Bert through the low doorway with a sense of coming home. From the time the boys had been old enough to take their places at the roundups, they had all three slept in the bunkhouse. It was Kate Donovan's theory that each one should be equipped to stand on his own feet, and she had never coddled any of them.

But the men about the square table under the swinging lamp were not the same. Ray Donovan needed but a single glance to tell him that. The old crew had been cowhands and nothing more — old-timers with a sprinkling of kids, men who spent their lives in the saddle, nursing the wide-ranging herds, fencing the water holes, riding the north drift fence, or salting the stock.

They had been quiet men, honest men, given at times to rough-house play, to a few practical jokes, but a friendly easy crew, many of whom had spent nearly their full life on the ranch.

Kate Donovan had always kept a big crew, but never the size that the ranch housed now. There were nearly thirty men in the square room, and something about them warned Donovan instantly.

They were toughs, gunmen. There was an uneasy watchfulness about them that spoke of lonely camps, of long, crooked trails, of sudden deaths. These were no ordinary hands, working for $40 and their grub. He had seen too many like them in the rough railroad towns. He had hired too many himself to help him clean out the vultures who swarmed around the head of track. These were hired guns.

Bert sensed his surprise and said in a tone that barely carried to his ears: "A nice crew."

Ray glanced quickly toward the younger Donovan and knew at once that Bert was expecting him to find trouble here and taking a certain relish in the thought.

He realized Bert did not dislike him, that in his own peculiar way Bert was really fond of him. But Bert enjoyed the thought of a fight, of any fight, merely for the excitement of the fight itself. Excitement was what Bert craved, what he lived for, to avoid the tedious boredom of the endless days, riding the ranges, watching the cattle, fixing the fences.

He said: "Who brought these lovelies in?"

"John," Bert said, his smile widening. "He likes his meat raw, does brother John. If he doesn't, how would you explain this bunch of merry cut-throats?"

They paused in the doorway, studying the big room. The bunkhouse, which had once been the main ranch building, was divided into two parts. The main room with its big stove in the corner was dominated by a long center table flanked by many chairs.

To the right opened half a dozen smaller rooms, each holding six bunks, three against each wall. In the old days the main room had been kept scrupulously clean by its group of careful bachelors. But now it was littered and strewn with gear, rifles, a broken saddle, a long whip with a frayed lash, a dozen dog-eared magazines.

The air of the place was close, a mingling of tobacco smoke with the smell of old cooked food and unwashed bodies. The men were for the most part unshaven, some of them downright dirty. The old crew would have escorted them forcibly to the creek. The old crew had been clean, with a personal pride in its appearance. This bunch simply did not care.

"Not a pleasant place," Bert said, still speaking under his breath. "I moved up to the main house when I came back."

Ray Donovan had no intention of moving up to the main house. He would not be welcome there by either John or Aunt Kate. But he did mean to do something about this room. Because men lived in constant worry of their back trail was no cause for them to exist like hogs.

He walked on in, trailing Bert. Every eye in the big room was on him, and he found no sign of friendliness in any bearded face.

There was little to choose among them. Several had been playing cards when he came in. Now the cards were forgotten, not one of them even making the pretense of continuing the game. It was as if he were a stray dog, pitched into the kennel of a closely integrated pack, and the pack was already showing its fangs.

Men of this type always regarded a stranger with hostile suspicion. It was entirely natural with their way of life. A stranger could well be a sheriff or a marshal, tracking them down for some former crime, or he could be a friend of someone they had mistreated or killed in the past. To join their tight-knit society, a man had to prove himself in their hard eyes.

He did not catch all their names. He did not even try. Names meant nothing to men of this type. He was willing to gamble that every man within those walls had changed his name at least once. Names weren't like brands. They could be blotted without leaving a trace.

"This is Kemp," Bert was saying. "He'd be a foreman if John wasn't acting as foreman himself. This is Ray Donovan, Kemp. He's joining the crew."

Kemp was a big man, standing as tall as Ray and a good twenty pounds heavier. He was hard bone and muscle, as hard and solid as a block of granite.

He extended a thick-palmed hand half-heartedly, saying nothing at all.

Bolger was a thin man with a scrawny neck and a prominent Adam's apple. He seemed inoffensive until you got a full look at his eyes. The eyes were so light that they looked like chalk, and they sent a shiver racing up Donovan's spine. It was something he could not quite understand. He had never been instinctively afraid of a man before.

Then came The Kid, young, with yellow down on his thin cheeks as if they had not yet experienced the touch of a razor. He was hatchet-headed and shifty-eyed, not a

146

person to let get behind you when a show-down came. There was an old man with a bare skull, called Baldy, and another with an equally bare head and a scarred cheek who answered to the name of Curly. A pretty outfit — misfits, small criminals, kill-ers — sitting here in the Box D bunkhouse that had once held decent men.

If Donovan had needed any more cor-roboration of his idea that there was some-thing seriously wrong at the ranch, he had it before his eyes. He followed Kemp silently into the side room and nodded as the straw boss indicated an empty bunk. He had no blankets, but Bert brought him some from the main house. He had no gear, since his duffel was still at the Dondaro hotel. He had no friends in this new group. Nothing was said as he came back into the main room, but he knew it more clearly than if the words had been shouted at him. He was alone.

It was not a new experience. Most of his adult life had been spent in loneliness in the middle of sprawling towns, for in his work he could trust no one but himself. He trusted no one but himself now.

Bert had gone. Both Kemp and Bolger had disappeared. The card game was re-newed — Baldy, Curly, The Kid, and two others playing. The rest of the men loafed about the room. Donovan knew that this was late for most of them, that ordinarily the crew would have bunked down long before this. But they were waiting for something. There was an air of expectancy about the place, a veiled watchfulness.

The door opened and Kemp and Bolger stomped in. Donovan had been sitting in the far corner, pretending to read a six-month-old magazine. Kemp looked around, and then tramped directly across to him.

"Thought I recognized you." His voice was heavy, challenging. "Saw you in Cheyenne, three years ago. You beat up a friend of mine, crippled him for life."

Donovan was certain he had never seen Kemp before. He seldom remembered names. Names were of no great importance; he also very seldom forgot a face.

But he was not surprised. The pattern was the same. It almost never varied. If Kemp had not used this excuse, he would have chosen some other. It meant a fight. The men in the room knew it, and forgot to pretend interest in what they had been doing.

He stood up slowly, studying his man as he did so. Kemp's shoulders were wide, his hips slimmed down by much riding, his heavy legs slightly bowed. He wore a pair of worn Levi's that were nearly black with dirt and grease, a butternut shirt, open at the collar to show a V of his hairy chest. His hands were large, knobby knuckled as if they had been broken in past fights. His nose was flat, and his broad cheeks wore a fringe of straggling, black stubble at least three days old.

But it was the eyes that held Donovan. Pig eyes, too small for the face they decorated, red-rimmed as if he had been riding for days in a dust storm.

If Kemp had expected that Donovan would duck this fight, he had counted wrong. Donovan had known from the moment he first stepped into this bunkhouse that a fight was inevitable. These men understood nothing but force and violence, and they respected nothing but brutality.

He set himself deliberately to punish Kemp as much as possible, and take as little punishment in return as could be managed.

With this in mind he struck the first blow. He drove his left directly into Kemp's grinning mouth. He felt the lips pulp under the blow and saw the glaze of pain that momentarily touched the red-rimmed eyes. And then Kemp was charging him with all the finesse of an outraged bull, both huge fists swinging at the end of his powerful arms.

He expected Donovan to cower away. Donovan didn't. He ducked his chin under his left shoulder and bored in, his left out straight, flicking toward the man's eyes, his right cocked and charged like a lethal stick of dynamite.

Kemp tried to beat down the left with main strength, and the next instant Donovan was inside, his chin hooked on Kemp's shoulder, both fists working like pistons on the man's ribs.

Kemp grunted from the body punishment. He tried to bring up his knee, but Donovan had expected that. He dropped his right hand, hooked the fingers under Kemp's knee, and stepped quickly backward, pulling the big man's feet out from under him and dumping him to the hard floor of the bunkhouse with a jolt that shook the whole building.

Kemp lay there for a minute, the breath blasted out of him, gasping like a dog at the end of a choking leash. Then he managed to roll over onto his stomach and come up to his hands and knees. He stayed that way for a full minute, looking across his shoulder at Donovan's boots as if he had never seen a pair of boots. There was no sound in the whole bunkhouse save the heavy breathing of the watching men.

Then Kemp rose to his feet. He was wearier this time, but it was very plain that he did not consider that the fight was ended, and that he could not understand why Donovan had not put the boots to him when he was down.

It was no feeling of fair play that had kept Donovan from kicking the prostrate man. In this game there were no rules. It was rather that he felt that Kemp had not had a severe enough beating to break his spirit, and unless that were achieved the whole purpose of the fight was lost.

He watched until Kemp stood solidly on his feet, and then he charged. Kemp tried to keep him off with a straight left, but Donovan knocked this aside and again drove his right into the crushed mouth. He took a blow just above the ear in return, and its force spun him half around. Kemp could hit, once he got himself set. Donovan danced away, fending off the man's charge in an effort to gain time to allow his head to clear.

But Kemp had changed his tactics now, and his enormous well of strength was pouring back into him as he recovered from the fall. He drove Donovan against the wall, and forced him along it toward a corner.

They went over a chair, both of them falling heavily, their big bodies breaking it to match wood as they rolled backward and forward in each other's arms.

And then Kemp was suddenly on top, his big hands wrapped at Donovan's throat, his powerful fingers biting into the skin as he attempted to shut off Donovan's wind.

Donovan felt his senses sway. A reddish film seemed to be drawing across his eyes. He reached up and tore at the circling fingers in frenzied desperation. Failing to break the grip, he arched himself suddenly in an effort to throw his opponent from him

Kemp clung to his place, like a man trying to stay in the saddle of a bucking horse. Donovan arched further, and then rolled suddenly, the movement catching Kemp unawares. He let go his grip and threw out a hand to steady himself, and Donovan, lying on his back, brought around a blow, the side of his hand striking the man just below the ear.

Kemp's head snapped sideways. He lost his balance and would have fallen over if his head had not struck the wall. In that moment Ray Donovan twisted free and dragged himself to his feet. His lungs were laboring like a pair of overworked bellows, and it seemed to him that he would never again have sufficient air. But he also knew that the paralyzing effect of his blow to Kemp's neck would wear off in a moment, that, if he meant to win, he must win now.

Deliberately, and with the care of a woodsman swinging an axe against a pine, he stepped in as Kemp came up, and drove one body blow after another under the man's heart.

Kemp's tortured face stared into his, and Kemp started a roundhouse punch that had little direction or bearing. Donovan was inside now, driving first a right and left and then another right to the man's jaw. It seemed to him that he had never struck harder in his life, that it was impossible for any man to strike harder, that his knuckles must burst at any moment. And still Kemp held his feet, his eyes glazed, rolling, almost senseless, blood trickling from the corner of his battered mouth. He pawed at Donovan like a sightless bear. Donovan knocked the fumbling arms aside. Measuring the jutting jaw, he hit it with everything he had.

Kemp went down. His knees seemed to fold outward, like twin jackknives, opening the wrong way. He dropped to a sitting position, the wall behind his massive shoulders supporting him, his head lolling as if his neck were broken. Then he slumped sidewise, one cheek pressed against the dirty boards.

Donovan turned. His fists had a swollen feel, as if his hands had been soaked in too hot water. The muscles of his forearms were sore from the jarring impacts, and he looked for a moment ruefully at a knuckle in the center of his left hand, wondering if he had split it.

Then he faced the men, reading various reactions in their faces. The Kid was excited, his narrow eyes glowing, almost like a cat's, the hungry curl of his slack mouth telling that he would love nothing better than to pick up the fight if he dared.

Bolger's pale eyes were unreadable. He seemed utterly unaffected, as if the fight and the punishing blows had hardly registered upon his consciousness. Baldy was grinning, a wolfish grin, but one filled with thorough enjoyment. The rest seemed sullen, a little cowed, their eyes shifting uneasily from the fallen man who had been their leader to Donovan who stood watching them, still drawing desperately needed air into his tortured lungs.

"Anyone want to take this up?" His words were flat, without inflection. It took all his effort to still his labored breathing so that he could speak evenly.

No one moved. Nothing stirred in the big room. The Kid's hot eyes lost some of their burning quality and dropped before Donovan's level gaze.

Bolger's white eyes resembled two vacant windows, but it was he who broke it up. "All right," he said, and there was something final in the words, something that no one was anxious to contradict. "Baldy, give me a hand with Kemp. He had an accident."

Someone laughed, and Donovan turned his head to see Baldy grinning widely as he came forward. "An accident." The man mouthed the words as if he found them both pleasant and amusing. He brushed by Donovan, stooped and lifted Kemp as though the battered man weighed less than a feather, and moved out the door with Bolger at his heels.

Donovan continued to watch the crew, but there was no sign of fight in them, no urge to test their strength against his.

For the instant he had gained their grudging acceptance. It was not liking, or friendship, but merely acceptance, and he was satisfied. He followed Bolger through the doorway and went around to the wash bench. Below him he heard the sounds at the big watering trough and realized that the two men had dumped the battered

Kemp into the trough, bringing him to with sudden shock. He heard the strangled sputter, and then the low, even curses as they helped the whipped man from the trough, and thought that it would not be bad treatment for himself.

Instead, he slopped water from the bucket into one of the tin basins and, heedless of the drops that fell on his clothes, dashed it into his face.

The water smarted in the cuts, stinging them but further clearing his head, and by the time he returned to the bunkhouse he felt nearly normal aside from the weight of tiredness in his arms and shoulders.

Kemp was sitting hunched in a chair beyond the table, his wet clothes piled in a heap at his side, his big body naked save for the matting of hair across his barrel chest. He looked not unlike a gorilla, slumped against the chair back, his long arms hanging slack at his sides, his eyes still dull, his face puffed, his mouth a purple bruise.

He lifted his eyes to Donovan without interest, almost without recognition, then lowered them as if he found something fascinating in his calloused feet.

Donovan gave him a single glance, then crossed to his bunk room. He stripped to his underclothes and rolled into the blankets. He was almost instantly asleep. It was a knack he had, this ability to relax completely when the time came, to put from his mind the worries and misgivings that had plagued him during the day.

VII

They rode in silence for two miles, letting their horses beat out the first morning friskiness and settle into the slower pace that the animals could hold. Bert Donovan turned his head and gazed at Ray, his eyes mocking as usual.

"So you had to stick your neck out?"

Ray's returning grin was forced. It had to be, his face moving stiffly and crankily after its contact with Kemp's fists. "I hadn't much choice," he said.

"It's a fine crew we have." Bert looked off to the distant mountains rising like purple shadows toward the fleece-lined sky. "A fine crew."

"How long have they been here?"

"A few months. Most of them have come in since I ran away."

"Why? Why are they here?"

"John."

They looked at each other in studied silence that Ray broke by saying: "I wonder that Aunt Kate let him."

"She's scared," said Bert. "She's always been scared of crowds and cities and people. That's why she stayed on the ranch when her brothers took off. And she's scared of the railroad. She doesn't know how to fight it."

Ray eased his horse into the approaching grade and Bert slowed his own mount, riding stirrup to stirrup. "Do you believe anyone would be fool enough to build a railroad through here?"

Bert considered the question carefully as they topped the rise and started down into the long sweeping valley below. "I don't know much about railroads," he said. "I've seen some built through some right un-promising country."

"But they went somewhere," Ray insisted. "A railroad doesn't make money unless it has freight to carry. A lot of freight."

"Then why should Wilbur Keats pretend he's going to build a road? What can he hope to gain?"

"Maybe he thinks Aunt Kate will buy him off."

"Far as I know he hasn't spoken to Kate for over a year. Still, he might be working up to that. Anyhow, Aunt Kate let John hire these saddle tramps with the idea that they'd fight the railroad men if they came in."

"That," Ray said, "is the craziest thing I've ever heard of. If anyone has enough money to build a railroad, they aren't going to be stopped by twenty-five or thirty brush jumpers, even if they are armed with Thirty-Thirties."

"That's the story," Bert said. "I got it from Marty yesterday. Marty is pretty upset. She always did worry."

"And you haven't been much help to her," Ray reminded him.

Bert gave him a mirthless grin. "You won't be much help to her, either," he said. "You thought you were playing it smart last night, didn't you, joining the crew as a forty-dollar rider so you could be on the ranch and watch things. Well, you aren't as smart as you think you are, my boy. John out-thought you, and so did Aunt Kate. They hired you, not because they trust you, but because they figure it's easier to keep a watch on your doings if they know where you are."

Ray grimaced. "And they don't trust you, either. Is that why they're sending us to the northern line camp, or are you being included as a kind of policeman to keep me in line?"

Bert shrugged. "I don't really care which

it is, as long as I don't have to sit around the main headquarters, listening to Aunt Kate tell me what a disappointment I've been to her, or John lecturing me because I don't take the proper interest in the ranch." He stretched. "It's a beautiful country, Ray, if it wasn't for the people in it."

It was a beautiful country. In all his travels across the frontier Ray Donovan had never found any country that appealed to him more. Here was a land of high mountain meadows, of rushing streams, of pine and aspen, a rich land, all controlled by the Box D.

It was, he thought, an empire rather than a ranch, an empire to be protected, to be guarded, to be fought for if necessary. He could understand Kate Donovan's deep fear at the coming of a railroad — any railroad, even without claiming the alternate sections along the right of way, would mean the coming of people, the invasion by settlers.

This part of the world was a kind of backwash, almost as wild and primitive as it had been when Kate's father first saw it forty-five years before.

No, he thought, if it were his he would want to fight for it, too. A sudden longing swept over him that he could not quite repress. It wasn't that he wanted the ownership of the ranch. He merely wanted to belong to it. Here he had been raised, and the rolling hills with their timbered tops, the rushing streams and the lush meadows were in his blood. He thought of the lonely nights he had spent in the noisy railroad towns, of the homesickness that had mingled with his deep resentment.

He had thought then that it was a yearning for Dondaro, and for the ranch house and the familiar buildings. He knew now that it had been a simpler, cleaner yearning for the land.

He glanced toward the man at his side. Someday this would be Bert's. And he thought with growing bitterness, Bert doesn't even care. The ranch actually means nothing to him beyond a property that will earn money, that will furnish him with the funds to drink and gamble, to travel and wander. Marty, he felt, loved this land almost as passionately as he did, and she would never be truly happy anywhere else. But would her love for the land clash with her feeling for Bert and the conflict with John? Bert would never be content to remain long in any one place. There was too much of the world he had not seen, too many places of entertainment that could be easily visited if he were free.

And as soon as Kate died, as soon as the money was in his hands, Bert would consider himself free. Freedom was something that was neither bought nor earned. Freedom, in its usual form, was something that certain people were born with — a lack of the sense of responsibility, a lack of understanding that other people's lives and happiness might depend upon what you did. Bert was that way. He would not change. Nothing that Ray could tell him would make him change. He might grow silent and resentful under criticism, but he would not comprehend it.

Ray Donovan sighed. It seemed unfair that Bert, who cared nothing for the ranch should have it, while he who loved each curving trail that led across the huge property had no more claim or right than Wilbur Keats had, or Sam Friend, or for that matter Kemp.

The ranch, he felt, would be all right. Bert would not manage it, but John would. Maybe Kate Donovan was smarter than he gave her credit for. Maybe Kate had studied her two nephews and figured it out for herself. By leaving the ranch to Bert she tied him, however loosely, to the country, while John would be provided for because no matter what else Bert felt about his older brother, he trusted him and had faith in his business ability to handle the property. Yes, Bert would be an owner, but an absentee owner for most of the time, while John, in his careful, plodding, mechanical way, would run the show as manager.

But Keats. He had been thinking of Wilbur Keats. What was the man up to? What was this threat of a railroad? What kind of complicated scheme was at the back of Keats's mind?

He puzzled over this in silence while their horses covered the next five miles. He found no answer, and wondered if after all he could be wrong. Perhaps Keats was promoting the road as a stock swindle, hoping to lure unsuspecting investors into putting up money that he would then embezzle.

If this were true, it offered no direct threat to the ranch, but for some reason he could not quite come to believe it in his own mind. He was frowning as they reached the top of the second line of hills, and paused by common consent to let their winded horses blow.

Ahead of them was a jumbled land, looking like a bed quilt twisted into a hundred upthrust folds by a troubled sleeper.

It was a land of small side cañons, steep, tree-shrouded hogbacks separating them, of little circular grassed sinks whose turf was soggy with the water seeping from the dividing rocky ridges. And then, far below them, almost at the head of the main valley, they saw the fire and the tiny figures of the men, looking no larger than toy soldiers in the distance.

Bert saw them first and pointed without speaking. Ray, following Bert's direction, saw the light smudge from the fire.

"Who's that?"

Bert shook his head, and the same thought was uppermost in both their minds. That fire and those men were in the direct center of the Box D range. No one not connected with the big ranch had any legitimate business in that whole valley.

"Rustlers?"

Bert shrugged. "I wouldn't think so. They'd have to drive out to the north. They'd have to pass the boys at the line, and the chances are they'd be seen."

"Not part of the crew?"

Again the shake of the head. "Too many. We've only got three line camps up here, one man at each."

"Railroad survey?" Ray Donovan could not really believe it, but he could think of no other reason for the camp.

"Let's go have a look." Without waiting

for an answer Bert swung his horse down the curving grade toward the floor of the valley.

Now that there was a chance for action, Bert Donovan was suddenly a different person. He raked his spurs along his horse's flank and drove forward at a speed that forced Ray to hurry to match. It was nearly three miles from the spot where they first spotted the fire to the camp and they made it in less than half an hour despite the rough footing and the lack of a trail.

The men about the fire had seen them coming long before they arrived and were on their feet, watching. Ray saw that there were six of them, and that they held rifles. He called his warning to Bert, but whether Bert heard him or not he had no way of knowing.

Without a sign that he had observed the rifles, he drove straight toward the fire, pulling up the horse only when its sliding hoofs threw loose dirt into the flames.

The men had scattered and one burly one who seemed to be the leader came forward angrily, holding his rifle ready.

"Men have got shot for less than that, mister."

Bert Donovan looked at him, at the men behind him, formed in a semicircle, at the transit sitting to the right of the fire, at the target, lying on its side.

"And men have been shot for riding this range." Bert hadn't raised his voice, but it held a tense deadly quality, unlike his usual bantering speech. "This is Box D graze, and we don't like strangers here."

The burly man seemed unimpressed. "This is government land," he said, "no matter how many of your damned cattle are running on it. And this is a survey crew for the Dondaro and Northern Railroad."

"You never stop, do you?" Bert's hands were crossed on his high saddle horn. "A dozen of your fellows were run out of here a month ago."

"You won't run us," the burly man said, patting his rifle. "We have orders to go through, and nothing will stop us."

Bert hesitated, glancing across his shoulder to where Ray sat his horse, quietly watching. Bert was not afraid, but there were six of them and they looked as if they would fight. "We'll see," he said. "You've had your warning. The next time it will be harder."

He swung his horse, and, as he did so, a rifle cracked from a pile of rocks to the right. The ball made a soft *wooshing* sound as it caught Bert Donovan squarely in the middle of the back, lifting him out of the saddle with shocking power.

He fell, slanting forward, having enough left to kick his foot free of the saddle as he went down. The horse spooked sidewise, then charged away.

The fleeing horse perhaps saved Ray's life. Even as Bert was falling, he swung his own mount, and drove off, keeping the riderless animal between him and the men at the fire.

Another shot roared out from the rocks, the bullet burning its way across his shoulder, tearing the shirt but barely touching the skin.

He bent forward then, flattened against the horse's neck, and raked at the flanks, to send the frightened animal ahead in a bounding, surging leap. He was headed directly for the wall at the cañon's far side. This put his horse at the rising grade, forcing it upward where there seemed no path that it could mount.

They made it somehow, the iron shoes striking sparks from the nearly bare rock. They climbed into the edge of the scrub timber, with bullets still kicking up their dust puffs below them.

Once in the trees he turned right, finding a shallow declivity that was little more than a wallow, and leading his horse into it.

He swung down, tethering the animal with one hand while he jerked the rifle free with the other. Then he crept back to the break in the trees and peered downward toward the camp. It was three hundred feet below him and a good quarter of a mile away. He was surprised to see how great the distance was. The frightened horse had moved faster than he had realized.

It was too far for a shot unless they charged him, and they gave no sign of even attempting it. But as he watched, a puzzled frown drew a crease between his brows.

They were breaking camp. There could be no mistake about that. One man was leading up the horses while the others packed the transit and the supplies. There was something familiar about the horse guard, even at this distance, but not until the man had lifted himself into the saddle and turned to scan the tree-covered ridge that concealed Donovan did Ray realize that the man was Sam Friend.

A sudden, great anger surged up through him. The shot that had come from the rocks had been fired by Friend. He knew it as certainly as if he had seen the man's heavy finger squeeze the trigger.

He stood up, unmindful of whether they saw him or not. Had he been mounted, he would have charged down the slope, even faster than he had climbed it, in an effort to come to grips with Friend.

That shot had been deliberate. At first he had thought that one of the survey crew might have lost his head and fired, fearing he and Bert meant to attack the group beside the fire. But Friend was not one who ever did anything on impulse. Friend was as cool and calculating and deadly as a striking snake. And Friend had fired at Bert. If the shot had been directed first at him, Ray could have understood it. After the beating he had given the man in Dondaro, he could expect little else from Friend.

But as far as he knew there had never been any direct trouble between Bert and Wilbur Keats's gunman. Everyone in the country had always liked Bert. He was popular at all the dances, in the bars and the gambling tables.

Nor was there a chance that the shot had been fired in error, mistaking Bert for him. They were nothing alike either in build or appearance, and Friend knew them both.

No, it was deliberate murder, and with a purpose behind it, a purpose so important to Friend that he was willing to delay his personal revenge against Ray while he fired his first shot at Bert.

Ray swore under his breath. They were riding down the valley now, too far for a shot to carry, riding out of Box D range. To him this was further proof that he had been right. He was not too important to their plans. If he had been, they would have made an attempt to catch him on the ridge. No, they had accomplished their mission. He suspected that it had been an intentional trap, but he wanted to make certain.

With this in mind, and the driving desire to see if Bert still lived, he retreated to his horse. Mounting, he searched for an easier way back to the valley floor.

He found it finally, a good mile to the westward of the camp. He dropped downward, turning east. Following Corbin Creek, he came to the burned embers of the drowned-out fire. For an instant he sat his saddle, staring along the valley, alert, aware that this might be a second trap, that some of the men might have circled back or even remained in the rocks, awaiting his return.

But there was no sign of anyone. He stepped down, leading the horse forward, keeping it between him and the rocks from which Sam Friend had fired.

He reached Bert's body. Squatting on his heels, he examined Bert quickly. Bert was dead. He wrapped the body in a blanket and slung it across his horse. The animal was tired, but it spooked a little at the unwelcome load.

Donovan mounted. Riding slowly, he cut down the valley toward the trail. He was fully convinced now that it had been a murderous trap. They were camped here, and they had a transit, but there was no sign of stakes. If they were surveying here, they had started from no benchmark, and were heading nowhere. It was not even a careful deception. The men executing it had been too ignorant or too lazy to care.

But they had chosen the site of the camp well. It was enough off the main trail to the northern line camps so that it might seem that they were actually running the survey for their grade, and yet close enough so that anyone riding that trail could not fail to see them. Perhaps they had hoped to kill both him and Bert and therefore had not bothered to make appearances look too realistic. But they had bothered to bring the transit, and unwillingly he had to admit to himself that his escape was probably not due to the speed of his horse but to the fact that the men about the fire had not meant to kill him. They wanted him as a witness. They wanted him to return to the ranch and to tell Kate Donovan that Bert had been killed in ordering off a railroad survey crew. It might even offer a defense for the crew members on Bert's death.

Certainly the land on which they had been camped was government property, despite the fact that it had long been used by Box D cattle. Certainly, if the matter came into court, the men would contend that Bert had ordered them off when they had only been engaged in running a lawful survey for a railroad chartered in Washington, and that the younger Donovan had been shot only in self-defense. It would be their word against his, six to one, and it would resolve itself into who had the most power in the court, Wilbur Keats or Kate Donovan.

All during the long ride back to the ranch headquarters he turned the problem over and over in his mind. Who would stand to gain by Bert's death? Not Wilbur Keats, at least he could not see why the saloon man should profit. John? He thought of the older brother. But how would John gain?

The horse was very tired, and the double load added to its fatigue. It plodded forward slowly, taking most of the afternoon to reach the ranch.

Even that was almost too fast for Ray Donovan. He dreaded riding into the ranch yard with his silent burden more than he had ever dreaded anything in his whole life. It was news that he would hate to bring to anyone, even Kate Donovan, but when he thought of Marty and her feeling for Bert, he went cold all over.

Yet there was no help for it, no escape. He rode into the yard as the sun was slanting down behind the western mountains. The crew had gathered at the wash bench, and Marty stood on the porch of the big house.

She saw him and started forward. Then she recognized the still shape across the saddle. She stopped. He saw her face set with shock. He wanted desperately to help her and he did not know how.

She stood frozen for a moment. The men behind the bunkhouse had turned to watch, and now several of them moved forward, drawn unwillingly, like iron filings to a magnet.

He had to speak to the girl, to comfort her before they arrived. But he had no chance. As he dropped from the saddle and took a step toward Marty, Kate Donovan pushed open the house door. Kate paused on the porch, showing surprise at sight of him. And then she took in the blanket-wrapped figure and her face set hard.

She came toward him then, not speaking. She moved the corner of the blanket so that she could see Bert's still features. Then she turned and all the hate and bitterness of the ages were in her eyes.

"Murderer," she said. "You'll hang for this."

VIII

He told his story calmly, without expression, without allowing his feelings to show. He told it to a hostile audience, and saw the disbelief in their eyes. It had not occurred to him that they would not believe him. It had not occurred to him that the surveyors might have let him escape because they hoped he would be blamed for Bert's death.

Kate stood in her black clothes, looking like a wind-blown witch. Her eyes were bleak, her mouth bitter. The crew had moved from the bunkhouse and was lined up behind her.

Kemp, his face red and swollen, leered at the man who had beaten him, and awaited developments.

John stood beside his aunt, looking like a banker who had just learned of the cashier's departure with all of the bank's funds. Even Marty showed no friendliness. The girl seemed stunned, as if unable to believe the accuracy of her eyes and ears. She was not condemning him, however. Ray was certain of that, and he took his only comfort from this knowledge.

Rather, it was as if Marty had ceased to live when she learned of Bert's death, or was suffering from a severe case of shock.

Ray spoke on doggedly, even after he realized that he already stood convicted in their eyes. "That surveying party was a fraud," he said. "They hadn't been camped there more than a couple of hours before we came along. You could tell by the small bit of ash from the fire."

Kate Donovan said: "I might have known." She spoke in a toneless voice as if the heart had gone out of her. "I should have listened to John. He didn't want me to hire you. He didn't want you on the ranch."

Ray Donovan looked at John, thinking how little he resembled his dead younger brother. There was no real grief in John's face, only a set purpose, like a judge who has considered the evidence and arrived at the verdict. "You always hated us," John said in his level voice. "But was it necessary to kill Bert?"

Ray didn't answer.

"Oh, I don't think you shot him yourself," John said. "If you had, I doubt that even you would have the nerve to come back here. What I think happened was that you made contact with some of your friends surveying for the railroad. You probably thought you could sneak away from Bert unseen, but he discovered you, and one of your men shot him in the back."

Ray studied John for a long moment in silence. Then he turned on his heel and started for his tired horse. John's words cracked at him like a whip.

"Where are you going?"

Ray said without troubling to turn: "Off the ranch. I certainly don't seem to be welcome here."

"Wait."

He turned then and was shocked to see the gun in John's hand. If it had been Kemp, or even Kate Donovan, he would not have been surprised. But John almost never carried a gun. John was not wearing a cartridge belt, and for an instant Ray Donovan wondered where the gun had come from. Then his eyes strayed to Bolger who stood at John's side, and noted the empty holster at the man's thigh.

John had reached across and lifted Bolger's gun. Ray said steadily: "What do you intend to do with that?"

"I haven't decided yet." John met his eyes squarely. "Until I do, get his gun, Kemp."

The man with the bruised face moved in to lift the .45 from Ray's holster. He grinned sourly as he did so and his bruised lips formed the words: "It will be my turn in a little while."

"Now lock him in the old store room," John said.

Marty, who had not moved since first realizing that Bert was dead, said suddenly: "No, no, please, John."

John paid no attention to her. He said to his aunt: "Take her in the house and keep her there."

Kate Donovan took Marty's arm. The girl tried to pull free. John said sharply — "Help my aunt, Baldy." — and the big man moved in to take the girl's other arm. She tried again to pull away, then, as if realizing that she could not cope with the big man, she plodded toward the porch in silence. The last Ray saw of her as he was led around the corner of the house was her white, strained face, just before she disappeared through the door.

The storeroom was built of logs and it had no windows. Except for two barrels of flour in the corner, and a sack of beans, the room was empty.

He had no light, so he examined his surroundings with the help of a friction match.

Then he sat down on the bean sack, lifted his hat, and wiped his forehead with his sleeve.

Sounds from the yard reached him faintly, attesting the thickness of the walls. He knew that escape from here was almost as hopeless as if he were locked in an iron cage. It was, he thought, a sorry end. Much better if Sam Friend had knocked him over with a bullet at the same time that he shot down Bert.

And then he stiffened, realizing that, although he had told them about the happenings at the survey camp, he had not mentioned that Friend was the actual murderer.

His first impulse was to leap to his feet, to pound on the door until someone came, to tell both John and Kate that it was Friend who had shot Bert out of the saddle, and therefore it must be Wilbur Keats who had ordered Bert's death. But he checked himself before he rose. He had nothing new to offer them. Any survey party would naturally be sent out by Keats. He sighed and stretched himself on the hard floor, his head on the bag of beans. Whatever happened, it could be no worse if he had some sleep.

He had no idea how long he slept. He roused and his first thought was that someone was choking him. He could feel the fingers across his mouth, and then he heard Marty's whisper against his ear: "Quiet, Ray. Don't move, please."

He relaxed. It was pitch dark within the room but a thread of light bisected the far wall and he guessed that it came from the crack beside the almost closed door.

He was a man who came out of sleep quickly, fully alert almost at once. "What is it, Marty?"

"You've got to get away." The words came so softly that he could not be entirely certain that she had actually spoken. It might only be the whispered demands from his own brain. He had to get away. He knew that without being told.

"You've got to get away." This time he could feel the stir of her breath against his cheek. "They're in the bunkhouse, drinking, and Kemp is riling them up. They're planning to take you out and hang you at daylight."

"How'd you get here?"

"They left no guard. They figured that you couldn't possibly break out. I've got a horse saddled down beyond the road. There's a rifle in the boot and a gun belt with your Forty-Five hung on the saddle."

He reached out suddenly in the darkness,

catching her slim shoulders in his big hands. Somehow his mouth found hers. Her lips were soft and yielding. She did not return the kiss for an instant, and then she did.

"Bless you," he whispered. "You'll do to ride the hills with, Marty."

He came to his feet. Not until he moved toward the door did he realize how stiff he was from sleeping on the hard floor.

Outside, it seemed almost as light as day after the blackness of the storeroom. He heard Marty refasten the lock and thought how surprised the Box D riders would be when they came with their ropes in the morning and found him gone.

The Comanche moon was a yellow saucer overhead, and he stayed in the shadow of the building, hoping that none of the drunken riders in the bunkhouse would choose the wrong moment to come out.

The girl joined him, moving quietly as an Indian, only the soft pulse of her breathing telling him that she was there. "The horse," she said. "I'll show you."

His hand closed tightly on her arm. "You'll go back to the house." He felt the freshness of her hair against his lips as he whispered into her ear. "If I'm found, I don't want you mixed up in this."

"What difference does it make?" There

was a note of fierce hurt in her voice. "With Bert dead, there's nothing here at the ranch for me. Take me with you. I can get another horse."

"Where?"

"Anywhere. It was terrible, up at the house tonight. Aunt Kate's grieving. I never saw her like that. She never let anything affect her before, but now that Bert is gone, she's suddenly an old woman. And John . . . John just sat there telling her it was her fault, in that smug, self-satisfied way of his. He said that if she'd listened to him months ago this wouldn't have happened. He said she'd kept his hands tied, but if she'd give him real authority, if she'd turn the ranch over to him, he'd make short work of this railroad scare. He said he was going to clean out the whole mess. She hasn't agreed yet, but she will, and I can't stay here if John takes over. I won't stay here."

Ray said softly: "You'll stay for a little while. At least until I can find a place to take you."

"Take me wherever you're going."

"I'm not going anywhere, yet."

She stared at him in the half light, trying to read the meaning in his words. "But you have to go. If they catch you in this country, they'll hang you, and you can't go back to

Dondaro. Wilbur Keats runs the town."

"All right," he said. "I'll head north to Coxville. But I'm not going to leave the country until I find out what this is all about. And not until I settle for Bert."

She caught her breath. "You won't be any safer in Coxville than in Dondaro. They don't think much of anyone named Donovan in the higher hills."

He knew that as well as she did. "I'll be all right," he promised her. "I'll be all right there as long as I have a gun."

He didn't wait for further argument. He took her face between his hands and kissed her lightly. "Don't worry, Marty. You aren't alone as long as I'm alive. If you need me, get word to Limpy. I'll be back here before you realize it."

He slipped across the yard, thankful that Kate Donovan would not allow a dog on the place. He kept as much in the shadows as he could until he reached the corral fence, then skirted it until he reached the road that led eastward to Dondaro. He found the horse, stomping impatiently at its tether.

Marty had chosen well. The animal was black, with plenty of bottom, not fast, he judged, but the kind that could keep moving at a steady clip for long hours. He fastened the belt about his waist, lifted the familiar gun, and twirled the cylinder. A minute later he was in the saddle and riding away down the twisting road toward the rim above.

Across the rim he turned northward on a trace that was so faint that, had not his memory marked every rock, he could not have found it.

The night air had a sharp chill, brought to the land by the downdraft that suctioned past him from the snow fields still showing white against the distant mountain crest. He had no jacket and he shivered in the cold wind.

The trail weaved its way across the high plateau, skirting the small valleys, always working its way toward higher ground. The timber turned more dense as he progressed, pines replacing the aspen, and growing heavier, great trees, thick and straight, their rough bark furrowed and seamed, their needled branches shutting out most of the light from the distant moon.

He loved this high land, and he had not seen it since he was a boy. He rode, not minding the cold now, savoring the clean, scented air that seemed to clear his head and wipe out all the jumbled trouble of the past day.

Here and there, on the north side of small dips that he passed, were patches of snow, crusted with dirt and the needles of the pines overhead. The air grew colder, and thinner, and the horse's gait slowed.

They came thus to the saddle of the pass and dropped over it, the trail now following a shelf below which the racing waters of White Creek fought and gurgled their way around the boulders.

The creek swelled as they descended, being joined by the north fork that cut down the side of the cañon in a trough little more than a cleft in the rocks.

And then the narrow cañon spread and he came out into the Hole, a round valley, circled by steep, timbered ridges that climbed toward the paling sky. Crossing its marshy turf, he dropped down into the main street of Coxville.

It was not much of a town, a dozen unpainted buildings below the weathered ore dump, while, above the dump, the graduated tin roofs of the old mill caught the first haze of morning light as dawn crept tiredly over the eastern rim.

The mill was long abandoned, the drift tunnel from which in the early days nearly a million dollars' worth of gold-flecked ore had come was caved in and water-filled. The town, which once had held some three thousand miners and their families, had burned, and the charred beams and metal roofs had been washed out by a dashing flood.

Only the unpainted buildings on the high hogback below the dump had escaped the leaping flames and the rushing water, and even these twisted structures were too many for the small population that remained.

Coxville was a cemetery of man's hopes and wild ambitions, a ghost town, still inhabited by a few hardy souls who refused to believe that the mountain that had once been thought solid metal could actually be worked out.

These men grubbed in a dozen shallow holes across the timbered slopes, grinding their small finds in crude, homemade stamps and washing the resulting sludge in the icy waters of the creek.

The town had always intrigued Ray. More than once, as a boy, he had ridden into these hills for the sole purpose of loafing on the dusty gallery before the one remaining store, and listening to the old-timers as they spun their yarns about the past glory of the place.

But even as a boy he had sensed that no one from the Box D was really welcome in this town. Still Bert and he had come here, time after time, to fish in the white rapids of the river, to explore the old mill, climbing along the girders high above the rusting machinery like a couple of chimpanzees, or venturing into the old tunnel, scaring themselves with tales of vulture bats and flitting ghosts until they scrambled back into the safety of the sunlit slope.

It was, in a sense, like coming home, like returning to his childhood to find it little changed, for the weathered buildings looked no older, the street no more grass-grown than he remembered.

But it was a rustlers' town. The men who lived here, or lived farther back in the hills and used Coxville as their headquarters and supply point, had always eaten their share of Box D beef. From time to time Kate Donovan had launched an attack upon the town, riding in with her crew, but each time they had been spotted long before they arrived and found the buildings deserted save for Limpy Dupont who ran the store, and his half-Indian wife.

Twice Kate had threatened to burn the place, but both times Bert and he had begged so hard for the old town that she had held her hand. The rustling, while annoying, had never been very important. The country to the north of Coxville was so rough that it would have been impossible to drive a herd of any size through the maze of twisting cañons and ragged peaks. The stolen beef was eaten by the town's inhabitants.

But he knew as he rode in that he would not be welcomed here now. At best he would be regarded with suspicion and watched closely.

He brought the tired horse down the curving trail and pulled up before the broken rack that ran along the edge of the grass-grown street before the Dupont store. Beyond it was the two-story hotel building, the biggest structure in town.

Once it had boasted forty bedrooms, but the second story had long since been abandoned to pack rats while Dupont and his family occupied the downstairs rooms.

There was no sign of smoke from any of the chimneys. Coxville slept and Ray Donovan sighed hungrily. He had not eaten since the preceding morning. He walked around the long building, found the back door unlocked, and let himself into the long kitchen. There was wood in the box beside the old range and he set about building a fire. Then, rustling up a side of bacon, he pared off half a dozen slices and set them to frying in a pan. Afterward he threw two handfuls of coffee into the blackened pot and sat down at the table, waiting for it to boil.

A cold voice said from behind him: "I hope you know what you're doing, stranger."

He turned. Limpy Dupont was standing in the door that led into the old dining room, a rifle cradled in the crook of his fat arm.

Dupont was a grotesque specimen. Not tall, he made up for his lack of height by the huge girth of his stomach. He had been fat when Donovan had seen him last, well over six years before, but he was far heavier now. His neck had almost disappeared under a series of chins that stair-stepped down until they merged with his chest.

He wore a dirty, short-sleeved undershirt that was tucked into the belt line of his butternut pants, but which threatened to escape, pushed outward by the sagging belly. His flabby cheeks were covered with a blackish stubble and his little, pig eyes seemed almost lost in the fat folds of his purplish cheeks.

Donovan grinned, thinking that he had never seen a more unattractive member of the human race in all of his six years of wandering.

"Hello, Limpy."

The small eyes narrowed with concentration, and the fat man limped a step forward. One leg was a good half inch shorter than the other, and misshapen by an ill-set bone that had knitted thus after a fall down a mine shaft years before. "Should I know you?"

Donovan's grin was thin. "You should if your memory's still working. You kicked me off your store porch often enough when I was a kid."

"Ray Donovan." Surprised recognition came in a rush. "Well, I'll be damned."

"You probably will be unless you've mended your ways."

The fat man let the nose of the rifle sag until it pointed to the worn floorboards as he came forward to stand against the far edge of the table.

"And what in the devil are you doing in my kitchen?"

The coffee pot chose that moment to boil over, and Donovan jumped for it. As he moved, the rifle barrel came up with surprising speed, and, when he turned, he found himself staring into the black muzzle. For an instant they faced each other, Donovan holding the blackened pot, then Dupont let the rifle sag, a sheepish expression stirring the dough of his features.

"Sorry."

"It's your guilty conscience." Donovan smiled faintly. "It's just that you've eaten too much Box D beef."

The Frenchman's smile held a certain wry humor. "It seems to have agreed with me." He indicated the bulging belly as he set the rifle against a chair. "I never expected to see you in these parts again, Ray. I heard you had real trouble with the old woman before you left."

Donovan didn't answer. He put a loaf of sourdough bread and a crock of butter on the table and dumped the bacon into a plate. "If I'd known you were going to get up so early, Limpy, I'd have got your breakfast, but have some coffee anyhow. There's plenty."

"Thanks." The Frenchman's tone was dry. He got two cracked cups from the cupboard, added a bowl of sugar to the table setting, and sat down. The old chair creaked under his weight as if its wooden pegs could not stand the strain. "We're honored to have you."

"Don't be," Donovan said, his mouth already full. "If I could have run in any other direction, I would have. I can think of other places I'd rather be at the moment." He went on eating and the fat man watched him in silence as if he realized that Donovan was starving and was polite enough to wait until he had wolfed his food.

After Donovan pushed the empty plate away and drained his coffee cup, Dupont said: "Running from something? I heard you made a name for yourself in the railroad camps."

"Running," Donovan told him. He had no intention of taking the fat man into his confidence. He trusted Dupont no farther than he could have hurled him.

"You've come to the right country," Dupont said. "You wouldn't be here because of the new railroad?"

Donovan had been constructing a cigarette. He stopped, the paper held in one hand, the small cloth sack of tobacco in the other.

"And what do you know about the railroad?"

The fat man shrugged. "That someone is crazy. They're talking about bringing it up through the pass."

"And then where?"

"That," said Dupont, "is a question none of us can answer . . . unless they mean to unload the cars and carry the freight over the mountains on mule back." He smiled slyly. "I thought maybe you could tell me, you being a railroad man."

"I can't."

"And how long do you expect to stay?"

"I haven't the slightest idea." He met the fat man's glance squarely as he said it. "That will depend on other people."

"You're welcome," Dupont said. "I've not forgotten the times Kate Donovan's men were set to burn us out and you and Bert talked her out of it. How's Bert?"

"He's dead."

A film, like a blanketing curtain, came down over the fat man's eyes as if veiling his thoughts. "I heard he'd gone away. Where did he die?"

"Over on Corbin Creek. He was shot by one of the railroad survey parties, yesterday." Donovan had wondered how much Dupont already knew of what was going on, but there could be no mistake about the man's surprise. It was wholly genuine.

"The best of a bad lot," the fat man said, and was at once embarrassed. "I forgot you were a Donovan."

"I'm not. In fact, it's Kate's men who are hunting me."

Dupont whistled off tune. "So. A fine collection they have on the ranch, and they call my customers brush jumpers. Things aren't the same as when you were boy."

He rose, inspecting Ray's weary face. "You'll be wanting some sleep. Take the room at the end of the hall, and don't worry about your horse. It'll be safely out of sight." He moved to a cupboard, returning with some blankets. "It's been some time since this hotel has had a guest . . . not since my father died, and that's twenty years ago this month. It was a great town then." He grinned ironically. "Who knows, it might be great again, after my friend Wilbur Keats gets his railroad built."

IX

It was full dark when Ray Donovan roused. He lay for a moment on the hard bed, trying to recall where he was. Then he rolled over, fumbled for a match, and located a lamp with a cracked shade on the old washstand.

There was no water in the pitcher. The room he occupied was thick in dust and some of the plaster had fallen from the ceiling.

He dressed and stepped out into the hall, carrying his lamp, and turned toward the kitchen door, under which a thread of light showed.

The room beyond was bright and warm from the stove, and cheerful with the smell of cooked food. Dupont's wife was washing dishes when he entered and two children in their early teens, a boy and a girl, were at the table, open books before them. They looked up and then away, shy as young animals, their dark eyes and straight hair testifying to their mother's Indian blood.

The wife was short, round, and friendly, and her eyes showed a hint of hidden humor.

"Limpy's over at the store," she said. "He said to feed you when you waked up. You want to wash?"

Donovan said he did and she ordered the boy to show him to the wash bench. The boy moved out of the door before him, silently, and pointed to the bench with its wooden trough, fed by a pipe from the river above. There was a dipper and a tin basin. The boy dipped the basin full and stood back, still silent.

Donovan stripped off his shirt. The water was cold and the wind coming from the snow above colder. He shivered as he used the towel. He re-donned his shirt and followed the boy back into the kitchen. There was beef and potatoes, beans and more sourdough bread. He guessed that the beef had worn a Box D brand and not so long ago. It was freshly killed and he smiled a little, thinking how angry Kate would be, especially if she knew that he were eating it.

The two children watched him gravely, never taking their attention from his face. He tried to draw them into conversation, about the books, about fishing in the river, about the old mine. He got no response.

"They're not much to talk," the woman said. "People in the hills learn early not to talk." She said it flatly, without intonation, almost without interest. Then she went back to washing dishes.

Donovan finished his coffee and rose. He hesitated for a moment, and then stepped through the rear door. Above him the hill rose sharply to the foot of the old dump and the outline of the mill was shadowy and hard to see against the dark timber of the slope above. To his right the store building showed its lights. The rest of the dying town was in utter darkness.

He turned toward the store and came in through the rear room. Here Dupont kept his surplus stock. There was a surprising amount and many of the cases had never been opened. He paused to look at some of the tickets and found that they had been addressed to a dozen buyers including the Cox mine.

This, then, was the salvage from an entire town, gathered by Dupont who had been too stubborn or too brainless to move as the town died around him.

Viewing the accumulated merchandise, Donovan thought there must be enough here to last Dupont and his two children for most of their lives. There were not many buyers left in the hills.

He went on into the main store and found a good dozen men present. He was surprised by the number, and then realized that the store offered the only meeting place for miles around.

A card game had been in progress around a table that obviously had been salvaged from one of the saloons. A barrel of whiskey with three tin cups sat on the counter to the card players' right. The rest of the counters, the shelves, and the floor itself were piled with a confusion of goods that ranged from bolted calico to mining tools and machinery.

As he entered, all action in the big room ceased. He let his quick glance roam over the assembled men. They were a nondescript lot, bearded and dirty. Some wore Levi's stained by the red mud of the hills. These miners had been grubbing in their prospect holes, and their heavy boots were caked and cracked from working everlastingly in water.

Others he knew to be riders, yet he doubted if any of them had drawn a pay check from a ranch in years. They were the brush jumpers, the petty rustlers, the wanted men who chose to live back in the tiny mountain valleys, taking orders from no one, living on the game they killed, the stock they ran off. These men subscribed to no masters and recognized no law. They asked little of life save to be let alone.

They were as scary as animals, and as suspicious. He knew that if his hand suddenly moved toward his hip, a dozen guns would leap into action, for every stranger in these parts might be a lawman, and every man in the room had something in his past that put him outside the pale of the law.

He was careful not to make a motion that could be misunderstood, careful to show no interest in the gathering after his first sweeping glance. He walked toward the front of the store where the fat man took his ease, resting one enormous hip on the edge of the low counter.

"Dupont, I'll buy a drink for the house."

The fat man nodded with no charge of

expression. "You heard him, boys. Set to it."

One or two nearest the whiskey barrel took tentative steps toward the row of tin cups, but a big man at the far side of the card table spoke without getting up: "I like to know who I'm drinking with."

Donovan measured him. He was used to sizing up groups of men. Often his very life had depended on his ability to pick out the natural leader and center his attention on him, for in any given group there was always one man, or two men, who the rest would follow.

The big man was the leader here, all right. He was huge, with powerful shoulders and extremely long arms. His head was big and round and covered with black hair that curled so tightly that it resembled a skullcap.

Dupont seemed to be enjoying the situation. He said: "His name is Donovan."

There was sudden, heavy silence across the room. Even the men who had been moving toward the whiskey barrel halted and turned. It was evident that the name Donovan was not any better liked in Coxville than it had been six years before.

The fat man had had his joke. He chuckled, then added: "But he's no friend of the Box D. At the moment the ranch crew would like to hang him."

The crowd looked at the storekeeper, then back at Donovan. The huge man grinned and pushed himself away from the card table. "Come on," he said. "What are we waiting for?"

The others trooped toward the whiskey barrel. Dupont winked at Donovan. "Looks like you've made some friends."

"I could use some," Donovan said.

Dupont shook his head. "Not that kind of friends," he said. "These men will listen to you talk, and maybe even play cards with you, but they want no trouble with Kate Donovan, or for that matter anyone else. At the first sign of gunsmoke they'd vanish into the timber and an army couldn't find them." He led the way to the barrel, drew an inch into a tin cup, and offered it to Donovan.

After his drink Donovan moved over to the deserted card table and picked up the shabby deck. The players joined him and the game went on. The stakes were low, the cards uninteresting. He played, not so much for relaxation as to take his mind off other things. He kept seeing Bert, pitching from his horse, and Marty, as she had stood beside him outside the storeroom. He had to do something about Marty — but what?

It had been years since he had faced a

problem that he could not solve by direct action. All his work for the railroads had been surprisingly simple and uncomplicated, a matter of timing and balance and sheer nerve. He had been like a ring fighter, jabbing constantly with his left, keeping the gamblers and the toughs who infested the railhead towns off balance. It was impossible to lick them entirely. There were too many of them. You drove them out of one town only to have them appear in the next; you closed one dive and three others had come to take its place by the following week.

His employers had realized that, and they also had realized that you couldn't expect an army of rannihan gandy dancers to labor in the dust and heat unless they had a place to find a woman or to wet their throats after the whistle blew.

It had been his job to see that only a certain number of joints were open, that they were run fairly honestly, and that the men were neither drugged nor maimed within their walls.

He had been successful because he had built up a personal reputation for toughness that made even the most hardened gunman hesitate to match shots with him. He had been successful because he had managed to make the saloonkeepers understand that they would be permitted to operate as long as they maintained a certain order in their places, but that they would be driven out if they crossed the invisible line that he had set up.

He had been successful, because he had an ability to judge how far a man could be pushed before he was backed into a corner where he felt that he had to fight, and he had been successful because no personal interest or feeling was involved. It was as cold-blooded and machine-like as the operation of the railroad itself, and he had all the power and the money and the authority of the railroad behind him.

But here things were different. His first concern, in fact his only concern now that Bert was dead, was Marty's welfare.

Marty's life had been pretty well set up for her. She and Bert were to inherit the ranch, and John was to run it for them. But now, with Bert gone, what would happen to her? He meant to settle for Bert's death before he left the country, and he meant to investigate this plan to build a railroad. But neither of these things would solve Marty's problem.

The girl disliked John. If it were not for that, he might have thought that eventually, when her memory of Bert faded, she might come to like the older brother. It would perhaps be the best thing for her, certainly the best thing for the ranch, and, since the ranch had always come first in Kate Donovan's thoughts, he had no doubt that Kate would try to foster such an arrangement.

The idea was distasteful to him. He thought of Marty, wild as an untamed filly, Marty with her quick sense of humor and her ready smile, tied to the humorless John whose every move was as carefully planned as if his life were played on a gigantic chessboard.

To hell with it, he thought. It wasn't his business after all. The Donovans could settle their own problems without aid from him. He shoved back from the table, suddenly annoyed with the cards, and went outside. The night was quiet and with the stillness that comes in high places in spite of the constant brush of the wind and the running murmur of the river.

It is a stillness deeper than physical sound, a stillness of the spirit itself, a world at peace. He thought of the men he had seen in the store, men who gained little from their grubbing at the hard rock and their petty thievery, but who had one thing the owners of the Box D did not have: comparative freedom from worry. They had sought this backwash of civilization purposely, some running from the authority of an angry law, many running merely from the complexities of life itself.

Without knowing why, he climbed the slope, crossed the shoulder of the old dump, came up past the rotting mill and only paused when he reached the mouth of the old tunnel.

In the moonlight the rusting tracks that once had carried the ore cars hung down from him, their supports rotted out, making a kind of iron spider web in the half gloom.

He sat down, and finding a blackened pipe in his pocket, he filled and lighted it. He never knew how long he sat there before he made his way back to the hard bed in the old hotel, nor did he know how long he slept.

The sun was high when he rolled out in the morning. The family had breakfasted, and the kids were gone. Dupont fed him silently and he stepped into the midmorning sunlight.

He knew he should get his horse and ride out, for whatever business he had in this country was not at Coxville. But he also knew that he was unconsciously putting off the decision. He had no plan, and felt no desire to make one. Sam Friend would keep.

Sam Friend would be waiting when he finally made up his mind to ride into Dondaro, and Sam Friend would die for Bert's murder. He had no fear of meeting Friend, no lack of confidence in his own ability. This was not the cause of his hesitation. It ran much deeper than that. He was unwilling to leave the country until he saw Marty again.

The girl solved this for herself. She rode down the town's street just before full dusk. She rode hard, and her horse showed plainly that she had maintained the pace for miles.

Donovan was alone on the porch when she pulled up. There had been three men with him when the horse's hoof beats stirred the echoes of the cañon above. But at this first indication of an approaching rider they had vanished, leaving him alone in what had once been the teeming center of a booming mining town.

By the time she drew in at the rail and swung down, he was on his feet waiting for her. He caught her as she swayed and grasped the saddle for support. "Marty, what's happened? Are you hurt?"

She shook her head. "Tired." Her voice had a flat quality as if she were concealing deep emotion with difficulty. "Tired, just tired."

Her face looked white under the blanketing trail dust. There were deep shadows beneath her eyes, and a tiny puffiness at the lids showed that she might have been crying.

He led her to the edge of the broken porch and forced her to sit. Then he got a cup of cold water from the pipe that filled the trough. He was conscious that Dupont's young daughter peered at them from the corner of the old hotel but he did not pay any attention, and the young girl was too shy to come forward unasked.

Marty Donovan drank the water thankfully but in small sips, knowing the effect of sudden cold water on an empty stomach. Now that she was here, now that the long, weary, lonesome miles were behind her, some of her natural strength and confidence was flowing back.

There was comfort in Donovan's presence and she felt as she had as a little girl when she had run to tell him of things in her small world that had gone wrong.

She had never run to Aunt Kate. It would not have occurred to her to do so. Kate Donovan was not a woman who invited confidences from anyone. Nor John, for John had been worse. John had been old the day he was born, a careful, scheming boy who had gradually taken over a man's work at the ranch long before his years marked him for such a position. Nor Bert. She had never gotten any sympathy from Bert. Bert had pulled her hair, and made fun of her for being a girl, and made her the butt of his practical jokes. She had known almost always that Bert loved her, but it had been Bert's nature to be a little cruel to those he loved best.

It had been to Ray she came, knowing that he would comfort her, knowing that he would not condescend to her because she was a girl, but would treat her as an equal. Never had he been too busy or too hurried to listen to her problem.

She had come to him now, realizing with her conscious mind that there was little or nothing he could do to help, but still clinging to the childish instinct that whispered that Ray Donovan could solve anything.

"It's Aunt Kate," she said. "She had a stroke, not an hour after you left. She can't move or speak. She simply lies there on her old rope bed with Juanita taking care of her. It's horrible."

She buried her head in her hands as if by so doing she could cut out the sight of the once powerful woman who was suddenly as inanimate as a lump of clay.

Donovan was too shocked to say anything for the moment. He had not liked Kate Donovan, in fact he had hated her thoroughly. But to picture the owner of the Box D as helpless was almost beyond his imagination.

Ever since he could remember she had dominated the ranch, and the region, and the men in it. She had been the ruler and at times her word had meant death or ruin to more than one man. . . .

"Can't she even write?"

"She's only half conscious, a kind of coma, the doctor said. He thinks it was the shock of Bert's death on top of this worry about a new railroad."

Donovan frowned. All this still did not explain Marty's presence in Coxville. She might not have loved Kate Donovan. But she wouldn't run away from the ranch if the sick woman needed her.

"What are you doing here?" he asked finally.

"I came to find you." Her face was again tight with worry. "As soon as Aunt Kate became ill, the first thing John did was to dig out her strong box and look at the will. I was in the room while he looked through the papers, but I thought nothing about it. I was too stunned to think of anything, and no one ever bothered to consult me about the ranch business.

"As soon as he finished examining the papers, I knew he was angry. You can always tell when John is angry. He doesn't blow up and lose his head like other men. He just gets more silent and that steel-trap mouth of his gets even tighter. I couldn't understand. He got up and left the house and I followed him to the front door. I heard him call Kemp and tell him to send a man to town after Judge Fox, the lawyer. He'd already sent one for the doctor.

"Kemp was still a little drunk. They didn't discover that you'd escaped until after daylight. Everyone was so busy thinking about Aunt Kate that they even forgot you were supposed to be locked in the storeroom."

"Go on."

She took a long breath. "Well, naturally I wondered why he was so upset. I went back and opened the dispatch box and right on top was Aunt Kate's will. It was short and simple. It said that the ranch was to come to me as soon as I married, and until that time I was to run it for the estate."

Ray stared at her. "No mention of Bert?"

She shook her head. "I guess it was Aunt Kate's way of punishing him for having run

208

off, of forcing her hand, of controlling him. If the ranch were in my name, I'd be in a better position to keep him in line."

"What happened then?"

"The doctor came. I've told you what he said. He thinks she might live for a while but that she'll never regain her speech. But she might die at any moment."

"Did the lawyer come?"

She nodded. "Half an hour later. He and John went into the big room and I listened. I thought I had a right. The lawyer read the will, and he told John it was clear enough. I was the beneficiary and with Aunt Kate incapacitated any court would make me her guardian and give me the power to control the property until her death."

"And John?"

"I've never heard him so angry. He cursed Aunt Kate for having the stroke before he was ready, and he said that no court in this part of the country would go against his wishes. The lawyer agreed, but he added that there was a simpler way . . . all John had to do was to marry me."

Ray Donovan swore silently.

Her voice became more strained. "They're working together. I don't understand every-thing that was said, but apparently John has a lot more power in this country than anyone realized."

Ray thought this over. It was not too difficult to understand. For years John had served as his aunt's deputy, with all the power of the big Box D behind him. In that time he undoubtedly had done favors for certain people, helped elect judges and the sheriff.

"They didn't catch me listening," she said. "Just then Kemp and the crew discovered that you'd escaped from the storeroom, and everyone got excited. I didn't see John until after breakfast, and then he accused me of helping you escape. I guess I lost my head then. I've never liked him and in that moment I hated him. I told him I'd not only helped you escape, but I'd read the will and overheard him and the lawyer talking.

"For a minute I thought he was going to strike me. Then he turned on that cold smile of his instead. He said he wasn't angry at me for helping you escape. He said he'd never had any intention of letting them hang you. He just had you locked in the storeroom to teach you a lesson.

"I told him I thought he was lying, and that I was going to Dondaro to see the court and get the judge to appoint me as Aunt Kate's guardian. He laughed at me then. He said the judge already had his orders and there was nothing I could do. He said the only way I'd ever see my share of the ranch was to marry him."

"But how'd you get away?"

"He didn't even try to stop me. I guess he felt that he had everything under strict control. I merely went down and had Baldy saddle me a horse and rode out. I pretended to head for Dondaro, but I circled back here. I wanted to see you. I wanted to ask you what to do."

He stared at her, wondering what she would have done had he not waited in Coxville. It had been his hunch to wait, although he had hardly realized it at the time. He had played hunches before, and they usually paid off.

"Stop worrying," he said. "He can't make you marry him."

"In this country I think he can. I haven't a friend in the world I can trust. The old crew is gone and the new men will take John's orders. I had no one to turn to . . . no one but you."

"All right," he said. "We aren't licked yet. You must be hungry after your ride." He led her toward the hotel kitchen. She was half through the hasty meal that Dupont's wife set before her when the fat storekeeper hurried in.

"I thought you'd want to know," he told them. "John Donovan is coming down through the pass and it looks like he has the full crew with him."

X

For nearly the full length of his life John Donovan had been convinced that he was better than the people around him. He could not remember when he hadn't looked with contempt upon the actions of his younger brother, and, as they grew older, this contempt had gradually turned to hate.

The hatred had been engendered by the knowledge that from almost the first day they had come to live at the Box D after their father's death, their aunt had preferred Bert to himself. John had been very conscious of her feelings and he had set himself to win her favor, not because he had any love for Kate, but because he had realized almost before he reached his teens that in the end one of them would be her heir.

With this in mind he had assumed a man's work, long before the ordinary boy would have given much thought to anything save hunting and fishing, and by the time he reached his twentieth year he had set himself up as the unofficial foreman of the ranch, and tried to excel in everything that he undertook.

He had no competition from Bert, who was too easy-going to be aware that his brother was attempting to outshine him. But in Ray Donovan he had been up against an entirely different proposition.

Ray naturally did things easier than John did. He was quicker, faster to learn, and he, too, was attempting to impress Aunt Kate, if only for the reason that he felt insecure because he was adopted.

John watched him, and, as he watched, his dislike of the other boy grew. He took out his ill feeling in bullying, in ordering Ray about until the morning Ray turned on him and fought.

He had taken a licking then, but the memory was softened by the fact that Aunt Kate had intervened in his behalf. Kate had whipped Ray and Ray had run away.

After Ray left, it seemed to John that he needed only to bide his time. He did everything he could to encourage the wild streak in Bert, feeling that sooner or later his younger brother would get into serious enough trouble so that Kate Donovan would be finished with him.

But the ways of women, he found, were strange. The wilder Bert Donovan became, the more both Kate and Marty appeared to love him, and as time went on it seemed that John's position became more hopeless.

True, he had become the real foreman of the ranch, gradually replacing the older men with a crew that would be loyal to him. He had needed something to scare the old woman into putting him in full control, something that she could not cope with herself. The idea of the railroad with its apparent threat of cutting the ranch in half had seemed perfect, and Bert's choosing to run away from home had fitted in nicely. For once Aunt Kate had been thoroughly angry with her youngest nephew, feeling that he had deserted the Box D in the time of the ranch's greatest need. She had gone to town at once, determined to change her will, and John had felt that at last he was making progress.

And then the lawyer, who was in his pay, had told him what the change involved. The ranch was not to be his after all. It was left in trust to Marty, to be turned over to her when she married.

John had known then that Aunt Kate, for all her anger at Bert, had not really changed her mind. He knew, as everyone on the ranch may have known, that Marty was in line to inherit.

He had not cared before. Women as such had never really interested him. His whole life had been an effort to outwit his aunt, to get control of the Box D for himself. But he set himself to be nice to Marty, only to have the girl rebuff his every advance. He had not worried, however. With Bert gone, with Kate Donovan becoming more and more concerned about the projected railroad, time seemed to be on his side.

Then Bert had come back, and worst of all Ray Donovan had been with him, a new Ray, certain of himself, experienced and tried by his work in the railroad towns. He had to move faster then. His first move had been to try to drive Ray out of the country. When that had failed, he'd sent in a message to Wilbur Keats and set up the scene for Bert's murder. With his brother dead, certainly Kate Donovan would turn to him. She could not leave the ranch to Marty, not with its being threatened.

But he had counted without Kate's stroke, without the fact that it was not physically possible for her to change the will, even if she wanted to.

At once he realized that his one remaining hope of getting the ranch was through Marty, but he had not been surprised when she refused him. He had not even been very worried. Wilbur Keats was in full control of Dondaro, and Wilbur took his orders from John. His main concern was that Ray Donovan had escaped, and probably was hiding somewhere in the hills. Ray Donovan was dangerous. If Ray chose to combine forces with Marty, they could still upset all his plans. The easiest way to find Ray was to let the girl lead him to Ray. Since she had engineered Ray's escape, she probably would go to him now.

So he had let her ride away from the ranch, and had given Baldy orders to see what direction she took. When she circled back and headed toward Coxville, he was sure she was going straight to Ray. Ordering the full crew to saddle up, he took her trail, careful not to get so close that she would realize that she was being followed.

He smiled as they rode. Kemp was at one side, Bolger at the other, the rest strung out behind them. He had picked all these men with care. Each one had been in trouble before coming to the Box D. Each had a record against him, some crime for which the law had not yet been satisfied.

They were his men, because the Box D stood behind them, because the big ranch would not hesitate to fight their battles as it would fight its own.

He had made this plain to each of them, not threatening, merely letting them know that he had taken the trouble to check back on their former activities. He did not have their friendship, nor did he want it. He considered himself above them, conferring a favor in letting them do his work.

Without them he would not have ridden thus to meet Ray Donovan. Somewhere, back in the dark recesses of his mind, he admitted to himself that he was afraid of Ray. He could not understand this, since he had never been afraid of other men. Perhaps it went back to the licking that Ray had given him six years ago. Perhaps it went back further than that, to the knowledge that when they were children Ray had always managed to beat him at whatever they both attempted.

But it would soon be over now. They were riding into the pass through the early evening air. Coxville lay on the other side, not five miles away.

They had Donovan cornered. There was no way he could run except north, and the mountains, still heavy with spring snow, offered little chance for escape. And Ray Donovan would not run. Of this John was confident. Something in Ray made him stay to face things, stay as in a like situation John would never stay. There would be a fight, and Ray would die, even as Bert had died. But Marty, what of Marty? He had not thought of her directly.

It would be too bad if Marty died, also, little Marty, with those big gray eyes that always reminded him so unfavorably of Aunt Kate's.

Too, too bad — but far simpler if she died before Aunt Kate did. Marty had no heirs, and he would inherit the ranch naturally as next of kin. A lot of things would be cleared up when he got to Coxville, a great many things. There was Dupont to consider. He had never liked the fat man, and Dupont's store offered a natural gathering place for the petty outlaws who fattened on Box D beef.

It was, he thought, time for Dupont to go. The man was hardly important enough to bother to kill. It probably would be enough if they burned the store and the old hotel. While they were about it, they might as well burn the rest of the ghost town. The place was an eyesore and served no useful purpose.

He looked at Kemp. The foreman's face still showed the marks of the beating Ray Donovan had given him. He wouldn't have to urge Kemp on. Kemp would go after Ray out of pure personal vindictiveness.

He said: "We'll slip into town without being seen if we can. They'll be at the hotel or at the store. There isn't anywhere else. Two of you stay in the street. Stop anyone who tries to make a break. Anyone in that town would be better off at the end of a rope."

They reached the divide and swept down the narrow cañon, the drum of their horses' hoofs beating out the sound of the rushing stream.

They swept into the old, wide, grass-grown street, and hauled up before the store. At Kemp's orders, three of them raced around the building to cover the back entrance of the hotel and store. The rest went in through the front door of the store with John Donovan and Kemp in the lead.

As soon as they entered the big, cluttered room, John Donovan knew that they were too late for surprise. They had been spotted. He had suspected it when he had seen no horses at the old hitching rack. He was certain now, for Limpy Dupont was alone in the store.

Limpy came forward with his strange, crab-like walk, his face a picture of amiable surprise. "Why, Mister Donovan, this is a pleasure."

"It's one you won't enjoy long," John told

him grimly. "Where are they?"

Dupont managed to look more surprised than ever. "Where are who?"

John Donovan swore at him hoarsely. "Marty and Ray."

Dupont spread his hands. "I don't know what you're talking about." He was standing behind the counter, leaning his weight forward a little on his knuckles. John Donovan reached out, locked his fingers in the front of the none too clean shirt, and used his free hand to slap the fat man hard.

"You've got one chance, Limpy. Tell me where they've gone, and I won't burn this rat hole. Don't tell me and I'll light up the damnedest bonfire you've ever seen in your life."

Dupont's small eyes seemed to grow smaller, and his flabby face looked yellow and old. His eyes went to Kemp and the riders standing silently behind the foreman. He found no help in their hard eyes. The tip of his tongue came out to moisten his dry lips.

"You wouldn't do that to an old man, now would you, Mister Donovan?"

John Donovan cursed him in a low, dangerous voice. "You've got three minutes to tell us where they are, Limpy."

The fat man's face sagged even further

until it seemed that his soft cheeks might dissolve and run down across his dirty shirt. "A man can't tell what he doesn't know, Mister Donovan."

John Donovan hit him again, this time with his fist. The fat man's legs buckled and he slumped down, keeping himself from going to the floor only by clutching desperately at the wooden counter.

His eyes glazed as his mind clouded from the blow. He shook his head in an effort to clear it, all the time cursing Donovan in a soft undertone that ran his words together until it was impossible to understand them.

Donovan stared at him bleakly with no more expression than if his mind had been the works of a well-oiled clock.

"Take a couple of men and look for their horses," he said. "They'll have Box D brands. Search the hotel and bring this fool's woman and kids over here. If we don't locate Ray and the girl by then, we'll stretch Dupont's spine a little. Maybe he'll remember then."

Kemp grinned, nodded to a couple of the riders, and went out. Dupont had shoved himself upright and was standing now with his back to the shelves that lined the walls. Donovan walked back to the whiskey barrel, knocked out the bung, and dumped the barrel onto the floor. The amber liquid gurgled out across the dust of the rough boards, forming a spreading lake that seeped around the legs of the chairs at the poker table. One of the Box D riders made a kind of protesting sound in his throat. John Donovan looked at him without expression.

"There'll be plenty of whiskey for you all when this is over," he said coldly. "Until it is, I want you sober."

One of the other men laughed. Kemp came back in. "I can't find their horses. They must have headed for the hills."

John Donovan swore. A second rider appeared, shooing Mrs. Dupont and her two children before him. "Can't learn nothing. The woman is as close-mouthed as her fat husband."

John Donovan walked over to stand in front of her. The two children pressed close to her skirt as if they found some measure of protection in their mother's proximity.

"You know who I am?" Donovan asked.

Her eyes showed that she did, although she did not speak.

"I've already told your fool of a husband that I'll burn the place down if he doesn't answer my questions. I'm giving you the same chance."

She stared at him as if she did not know

what he was talking about. He watched her for another minute, then turned savagely to Kemp. "Get a rope," he said.

One of the riders went out to his horse for a rope. The woman and children watched John Donovan, never taking their black eyes from his face. It was as if they were hypnotized by his appearance. Their stares made John Donovan nervous.

He turned his back on them and walked over to face Dupont. The fat man had regained some of his composure. He stood silently as they put the noose around his neck. There was a hook, set in one of the ceiling rafters, and they tossed the rope over the hook. Then John Donovan, as if he derived a certain pleasure from doing so, took the rope himself.

"All right," he said. "Your last chance."

Dupont stared at him stonily. Donovan jerked the rope tight. He pulled, raising the fat man until Dupont's toes barely touched the floor. The children were sobbing. The wife said suddenly: "Why should I let you kill him? Those two never did a thing for us. They're hiding in the old mill."

Dupont's face twisted at her words, but he could not speak because the rope was holding his chin too high. Donovan gave the rope end another jerk, and then released it. He said — "Come on, let's get them!" — and led the way through the rear door.

XI

Hiding in the old mill, Ray Donovan watched the riders pull up before the store and disappear inside. He saw Kemp and the men come out and search the stables, then saw Mrs. Dupont and the children being led across to the store.

Behind him, Marty shivered. "I never saw anything like the way those people in the store disappeared as soon as they heard that John was coming."

Ray grinned in the darkness. "Every one of them has plenty of reason for making himself scarce, believe me."

"I'm sorry," she said. "I led them right to you. I should have realized John wouldn't let me get away so easily unless he had a good reason."

He didn't answer. John Donovan had appeared in the lighted rear store doorway, trailed by his men.

"Dupont sold us out," he said. "We've got to move quick."

"Where?"

That was the question — where? They had led the horses up the twisting old road to the mine tunnel and concealed them beyond the entrance. But the road ended at the tunnel mouth and the mountain rose a good four hundred feet above it, the face much too steep to be climbed by any horse.

"You'll have to get out," he said. "You can't take the horses. Get up to the top and hide there. They won't find you in the darkness. If I don't come by morning, you can slip back down to the store. Dupont will help you get out of the country."

She said quickly: "Aren't you coming?"

"No. I'll stay here and give our friends something to think about."

"Then I'll stay, too. I can still handle a gun."

He caught her shoulders in the darkness. "Listen to me. I'll be safer without you. If I'm alone, anything that moves is an enemy. If you're with me, I'll have to be careful not to hit you."

She was not quite convinced but he gave her no time to argue. "Go on, get up to the top of that hill and stay there. If anyone gets close to you in the darkness, shoot first and ask questions afterward. It won't be me. I'll give you full warning before I come."

She went then, and Ray Donovan stayed, watching the men climb slowly toward him. The moon was out, sailing through patches of cloud like a golden ball, at one second lighting the old dump below him plainly, at another obscuring it in darkness.

The men had spread out in a long, fan-shaped line, like skirmishers moving in for an Indian attack. They expected him to shoot and were keeping what cover they could.

His only purpose was to delay them, to distract their attention so that the girl would have plenty of time to reach the top of the hill. Once there, he felt that she would be fairly safe. The timber was heavy, and she could hear them climbing toward her long before they reached her.

But he did want her to have time enough to gain the top, and with this in mind he clambered to the framework of the old building and worked along it to the small window at the end that overlooked the dump.

The moon chose this moment to shine out from behind its sheltering cloud, as the cloud moved ahead of the stiff upper wind. The yellow light stripped the dump of its protecting shadows.

Now Donovan had a clear look at the men below. John had paused at the lower edge of the dump and was looking upward. The riders, still in their fan-shaped formation, were climbing up the slanting sides. The sides were so steep that they had to bend nearly double and use their hands in their ascent.

He lifted the gun from his holster and snapped a shot at John Donovan. The distance was too great to hope for a hit with a short gun, and he missed as he had expected to. The bullet kicked up dirt at John's feet, and John ducked for the cover of the store wall.

The men came on, swinging up both sides of the dump. He fired. He heard a long low yell as his bullet found its mark, and then the patchwork of clouds drifted across the moon, wiping out its light as if it had never existed, casting the whole face of the dump into darkness.

Under cover of the deep shadow he heard their voices as they shouted to each other. "They're in the mill! Don't let them get away!" And bullets whanged against the sheet-iron walls, their pinging like the buzz of angry bees.

Ray Donovan knew he could not afford to be caught in the mill. They would work him down into a corner and kill him as they might butcher a beef. He backtracked along the rafter and dropped to the floor at the upper end, then worked his way down through the darkness past the rotting sludge tanks.

He had an idea now. He did not want to retreat farther up the mountainside and thus draw them toward Marty's hiding place. He meant to slip through the old ore chute below the crusher and out through the opening that had carried the sludge to the dump beneath. Once there, if the cloud held its place across the moon long enough, he might manage to slip through their line and down the dump. If he were discovered, he still had the advantage: they would have to be careful with their cross-fire to keep from hitting their friends, while he would be free to shoot at anything that moved.

He found the opening. It was clogged with débris. Water had run into the mill from above, picking up loose boards and trash, and in seeking an exit had almost blocked the hole.

He dropped his gun back into its holster and tore at the obstruction with his fingers, trying to make as little noise as possible. He had to get out that way now or he was trapped inside the mill — for in the time he had wasted they had climbed to the level of the old building.

He grasped the end of a board and pulled it loose. He tore off a second and a third.

He tried to wiggle through, feet first. It was a tight fit. For one long, paralyzing minute he feared that he would stick there and that they would find him, helpless, caught like a rat in a trap.

Then he was through, dropping five feet to the top of the dump. He could hear the scuff of their feet as they climbed on each side of him in the darkness. He sat for a moment, listening. Then with his gun in his hand he worked his way down the side of the slanting slope, sitting like a child, sliding as if the weathered slimes had been a mound of snow.

Above him he heard a call. Kemp was demanding that he come out of the mill. There was a shot in the darkness, another, and then a third, the bullets pinging against the metal sides of the old building.

He paid no attention. He reached the bottom and moved on silent feet across the intervening ground toward the rear of the store. He had no clear plan. Vaguely he thought to get one of Dupont's horses and ride out, shooting as he went to attract their attention away from the girl above, to lead them back over the pass away from Coxville.

He stepped through the store doorway. He saw Dupont behind the counter, and then he turned.

John Donovan stood not three feet from him, with his back to the rear wall, facing Dupont and Dupont's wife, with the kids still clinging to her skirts. He saw the children's dark eyes roll with fear until little save the whites showed, and then he gave his full attention to John.

They were too close to use their guns. Ray would not have used his anyhow, because of the woman and the children in the room.

Obviously John was as surprised as Ray. His gun was in the holster at his belt and he made no effort to pull it. Instead, as if by reflex action, his right fist swung directly for Ray's chin.

There was a quick, hot satisfaction in Ray Donovan as he stepped inside the blow. He ducked his head just enough so that the fist brushed along the tip of his ear. He drove his left deeply into John's stomach. His right still held his gun and it never occurred to him to use it.

He dropped the gun, hearing it clatter on the old boards. His full attention was on the man in front of him. His blow to the stomach had bent John almost double. John grunted, the air whooshing from his parted lips, his eyes glazing with quick pain.

John locked his arms around Ray. It was a

protective effort, an effort to get in close, to hang on until his brain cleared. He was groggy, pain-wracked, but very strong.

Ray tried to break the grip. He swung around, taking the heavier man with him. He tripped over one of the chairs at the poker table, then slipped in the puddle of whiskey on the floor. He and John went down together heavily.

But the fall broke John's grip and Ray rolled sidewise. His head struck the front of the counter, a stinging blow that tended to clear, rather than mist his senses.

Dupont had waved the woman and children out through the front door at the start of the fight. He picked up a shovel from the collection of stock beside the door and made his waddling way purposefully back along the store. His little eyes burned hot with rage. He only wanted the chance to beat John Donovan's brains out of his head.

John saw him coming. Somehow John struggled to his feet. He tried to draw his gun but Dupont caught the motion. He swung the shovel in an underhand throw that carried it toward John Donovan, blade first.

Donovan ducked, dropping to one knee and pulling the gun as he fell. The shovel sailed over his head, swinging a little. Its handle struck Ray across the bridge of his nose as he came up.

It stopped him for a second. In that second, John Donovan got his gun free and began pumping bullets into the oncoming fat man.

Dupont stopped, a look of utter surprise in his little eyes. He put both hands across his stomach. They covered the ring of holes that John Donovan's bullets had made, but they didn't stop the blood that was jetting out in tiny streams.

Dupont didn't fall. He sat, almost as if he expected a chair to be under him. But there was no chair. He went down, all the way to the floor, his body a hunched, grotesque shape that seemed to straighten in a convulsive action until he went over to lie flat on his back.

It was as if Dupont had found the sitting position uncomfortable and decided to lie down. But Dupont had decided nothing, really. Dupont was dead.

The blow from the shovel handle had stopped Ray Donovan from saving Dupont, but it had not put him out of the fight. He was on his knees now. He reached out and got one arm around John's throat. He jerked John's head back, almost breaking the neck.

He held John thus while he chopped at

the side of John's face with his free fist. He struck in a frenzy, thoughtlessly, angrily, shocked by the killing of the storekeeper. He felt John go limp. He came to his feet. His gun lay beside the card table. He caught it up and shoved it into his holster. He sprang toward the counter, jumped it, and found a shotgun in the corner.

He scraped a box of shells from the shelf, ripped the gun open, and loaded both barrels. Then he blew out the big light, plunging the store into darkness, and ran from the front door.

The Box D crew was sliding down the dump, shouting to each other as they came. The moon had again retired behind its bank of clouds and the night was as dark as a mine pocket.

He raised the shotgun and fired both barrels in the general direction of the dump. He had no real hope of hitting anyone. His main object was to make as much noise as he could, but a startled yelp from above told him that one of the pellets had been lucky enough to find a mark.

He broke the gun quickly, thrust in two more shells, raised it, and fired again at the darkness. This time he drew half a dozen shots in return. He dropped the gun and ran down the road and around the corner of the old hotel.

They were converging on the store building. He heard several voices call John Donovan's name. He heard Kemp above the rest.

"The louse got John! Cut him off! Cut him off! A hundred dollars to the man that finds him!"

Ray sprinted along the side of the hotel and found himself at the right of the dump, close to the old road that curved upward to the mine entrance. He climbed it rapidly. Below him a light came into view as someone relit the store lamp. There was no light in the hotel. He wondered what had happened to Mrs. Dupont and the two children. He hoped they had gotten clear of the town. He reached the mine entrance and ducked inside. The stomping of the nervous horses told him that they were still safe. He came outside and began to climb the slope above the mine, calling softly as he neared the top: "Marty, Marty."

Her answer reached him, her words tumbling out in a rush of relief. "Ray, you're all right. You're all right. I heard the shooting and I was scared . . . I almost came down to see."

"I'm all right." He was at her side now and she came into his arms, her slight body trembling. "I didn't know. If something had happened to you . . . is John . . . ?"

He said grimly: "John's all right, unfortunately. I suppose I should have killed him."

She shivered again at his tone.

"It's funny," he said, "the way a man's mind works. I had him on the floor and I could have killed him. He wouldn't be the first man I've killed."

"Ray, don't."

"With him dead your troubles would be over. But I couldn't shoot an unconscious man, even if he had just murdered Dupont."

She caught her breath at that. "Dupont, dead."

"Very."

"Oh, Ray . . . his wife, and those children. They helped us. They wouldn't have been in trouble except for us."

He said: "Dupont was always in trouble. If it hadn't caught up with him tonight, it would have another night. A man can't be on two sides of the fence, Marty. He knew his customers stole Box D beef. He knew most of them were wanted in a dozen places. He knew that he had to take the chance of being with them."

"I feel sorry for him," the girl said. "His family built that store and that hotel when this camp was a roaring mining town. He stayed after the others had left. He sold to whom he could. Don't be so hard, Ray. There is a little good in almost everyone."

"In John?"

"Yes, even in John, I guess. I hated him. I still hate him, but I think I understand him better than you do. He loved the ranch. He wanted the ranch, and you have to admit that he worked hard and faithfully for Aunt Kate. And he got small thanks for all his work. She preferred Bert, just as I preferred Bert, but Bert hadn't earned the ranch. Even I have to admit that."

He said, with an air of mild surprise: "Marty, you've developed into quite a person."

She ignored the remark. "I know how John felt because I love the Box D, too. It was the one thing I could never forgive in Bert, his lack of interest where the ranch was concerned. The only thing he cared about it was the money it brought him. Aunt Kate knew that, I think. Aunt Kate knew that if she willed it to him directly, he'd probably sell it and go East or to Europe, or some place where he could play. But I must sound like a fool, talking to you this way. After all, it's only a piece of land."

He said soberly: "Not a fool. I loved it too, Marty. I think that's what hurt me the worst when Aunt Kate told me that I wasn't a Donovan. I'd never thought of owning the ranch for myself. I knew it would go to John and Bert and you when Aunt Kate died, but I had never given much thought to her dying. She seemed as healthy as a horse, as ageless as these mountains. I never thought of owning it, but I did want to feel that I belonged here. If she hadn't said what she did, I'd have probably been content to stay here for the rest of my life, drawing the wages of an ordinary rider."

She was peering at him in the darkness, but she had no chance to answer. Suddenly, below them, flames blossomed up into the night. Donovan pulled her back into the concealing trees.

"The fools have fired the store," he said.

Next, the squares of the hotel windows lighted up. In a moment the old curtains caught fire and the flames leaped out, clawing hungrily at the weathered boards.

The girl stared downward, her slim fingers biting tensely into Ray's arm. "Can't we do something, Ray?"

He knew that she did not actually mean the question. It was a reflex protest against the useless destruction. In the flaring light he saw the Box D crew, gathered across the wide, grass-grown street. They were staring upward, using the burning buildings in an effort to locate him and the girl.

And then a diversion broke across the night. Rifle fire came from the far ridge and from the upper end of the cañon. He counted at least ten guns and heard the girl say in quick surprise: "Who is it?"

"The mountain men, taking a hand. They don't like seeing their store burn."

Below them, the Box D crew had been caught flat-footed by the unexpected attack. Bathed in the bright light from the burning buildings, they made perfect targets for the hidden riflemen.

They turned, looking about desperately for cover, and two of them ran around the angle of the burning buildings. Ray pulled his gun and fired down upon them. It was much too far for anything but a lucky hit with a short gun, but his shots threw them into further panic, and they made a sudden wild dash for their tethered horses.

One man went down in the middle of the street, a second, and then a third. The rest gained the horses and were swinging up. They did not bother to return the fire. There was nothing to shoot at, only the dark line of the trees, rimming the cañon.

They fled, driving their horses toward the pass, not even stopping to see whether their downed friends were dead or merely wounded.

It was a strange crowd that gathered before the still burning buildings in the grass-grown street. The roof of the hotel had just fallen in, sending up a fountain of sparks that reminded Donovan of a 4th of July celebration he had once seen in Denver.

There were some twenty men in the street, all armed. He thought that if they had shown fight earlier, they could have driven the Box D crew back across the pass before real trouble started. But these men avoided trouble by instinct, and there was nothing in their natures to bind them together. They were outlaws, but more than outlaws they were individualists, going their own ways, taking orders from no one.

They had retreated to the hills at the first sight of the Box D crew, and they would have remained out of sight until the crew rode away. They would not have come out to assist him, nor would they have raised a gun to help Marty. But they had started shooting when the store was fired. They had done this out of individual anger, for the store offered the only source of their small comforts, their only center of activity.

Ray and Marty made their way down to what was left of the town. Marty, seeing Dupont's wife and children, went over to comfort them. The big man who Donovan had noted at the card table as a natural leader voiced the sentiments of the outlaws. "Damn the Box D." He was talking to no one in particular. "I'd shoot John Donovan if I could get my hands on him."

At these words, Marty walked over to face the group of men who stood uncertainly watching the still burning buildings.

"Do you mean that?" she demanded.

Ray blinked in surprise. This was not the girl he had known. This was a woman who had suddenly grown up, who had the note of authority in her voice, the sureness of command in her carriage.

"Why, ma'am. . . ." The man who had spoken was embarrassed. "I guess maybe I did. There was no call for Donovan to burn out the store and kill Dupont. Sure, maybe we stole some of his beef, but he had so many that what few we butchered couldn't make much difference to him."

She brushed this aside with a little gesture of her hand. In the firelight she was a striking figure, straight and purposeful and un-afraid.

"All right. I'm Martha Donovan. The ranch is willed to me and my aunt is paralyzed. John Donovan has no more right on the Box D than any of you do. How would you like to work for me?"

They stared at her, not knowing quite what to say. This girl looked no more than an overgrown child, but there was nothing child-like in her manner, nothing vacillating. They sensed the purpose in her, and the hard resolve.

But they did not trust her. They trusted no one, not even their own companions. Ray Donovan knew that the plea was hopeless as soon as Marty made it. He had taken the exact measure of these men the first night he saw them in the store.

At the moment they were outraged. Had the Box D crew stayed to fight beside the burning store, they would have battled John Donovan's men. But the high point of their anger was already past, dying slowly, like the fire that still licked at the charred timbers of the two buildings.

By tomorrow morning the blaze would be nothing but a white heap of cooling ashes, and these men would have scattered to their various camps. They were not the type who made a fighting crew. They were lone operators, petty in their wants and desires.

He saw that the knowledge of this was flooding in on the girl. He took her arm then and led her aside.

He said — "It's no use, Marty." — in a quiet, reassuring tone. "Even if they agreed to ride with us, they wouldn't stay when the chips were down. Their bullets killed three Box D men tonight, and they won't forget it. They would constantly remember those men, and the specter of possible revenge from the ranch crew would ride with them always. They'll think about it tonight, and maybe tomorrow, and one by one they'll take their horses and slip away. There are other mountains in the country, other hideouts not quite as close as this to a vengeful ranch."

"You knew that before I spoke?"

He nodded and her voice gained a little helpless note. "But, Ray, what are we going to do? We can't fight John all by ourselves. He's too strong. He has too many men. He practically runs this part of the country."

He said: "We aren't any worse off than we were a while ago before you asked those men to help."

She sighed sadly. "I suppose that's right, but when I saw how angry they were, how their shots had driven John and his men away, I took hope. I thought we could recruit a crew. I thought, with them at our backs, we could ride in and take over the ranch. We could go into Dondaro and force the courts to recognize my claim."

"The ranch means the world to you, doesn't it, Marty?"

"But of course. You know that. You told me it also meant a great deal to you."

"I was thinking aloud," he told her. "The smart thing for me to do is to get out of this country. I won't try and minimize the danger to you. If I know John, he'll stop at nothing to get control of the Box D. It's an empire and in his own way he feels it's rightfully his. I suspect he wouldn't even hesitate to kill you if he thought it was his only way to gain his end."

She nodded.

"You and I might manage to slip out northward through the mountains. The snow is deep on top and we might never get through. But the chances are that we would. They're building a new road down in Texas. I've already been approached. I can get a job there and make enough to take care of us for the time. Then we might recruit a crew and come back here."

"And in the meanwhile John would have consolidated his position."

"Yes. That's true."

"I'm not going to run away," she said. "I'm going to stay and fight. I told Missus Dupont that, if I get back the ranch, she and the children have a home there for as long as they wish. It was the least I could offer. But first I've got to win that home."

He didn't answer, and she tried to read the mask of his face in the dying firelight. "But this isn't your fight, Ray. I dragged you back here, asking you to bring Bert home."

"It was my chance to come home, too," he said. "The first real excuse I'd had in six years."

"And you'll stay?"

"Of course. I never really meant to do anything else."

"Thank you," she said, and, before he realized what she meant to do, she lifted herself onto her toes and kissed him, hard, on the mouth.

XII

They camped at daylight in the timber beyond the pass, in the shelter of a high ridge from which they had a clear sweep of the long valley below. Donovan took the first watch, pulling a blanket from the horse's back and spreading it for the tired girl. She lay down, smiling up at him for a moment, and was suddenly asleep.

He led the horses down to the small

stream that rushed its way between the rocks and watered them. Afterward, he set the picket lines and climbed back to the ridge. He did not want to lose the horses but he would much rather they were discovered by John's searchers than have the Box D men stumble onto himself and the girl.

He knew there would be a search. John was too thorough a person to overlook the obvious. John had failed to corner them in Coxville, but undoubtedly John had left a man, hidden in the timber beside the pass, to watch for them.

For that reason he had led the girl up over the high crest, following an old trail that he had not ridden since he was a boy. The going had been rough, with the snow on the crest still deep, and it had been very cold.

Both of them had been near exhaustion before he finally called a halt. But even though John's man had missed them in the pass, Ray knew that Donovan would not halt his efforts. They had only two choices — try to get through the jumbled wilderness of the higher mountains to the north, or cut south and out through Dondaro.

No one in his right mind would attempt the mountains this early in the year. Even in midsummer the higher peaks held their constant caps of snow, and quick blizzards could develop, sweeping downward with unbelievable ferocity to bury the struggling traveler in a blanket of white.

No, John would be sure that they would make their try for escape to the south, and his crew would be in the hills, watching.

Ray wanted to be certain that he saw them first. He lay on the crest of the ridge, peering through the thin timber at the slope below, at the long stretch of the curving valley, and at the distant ridge.

He was hungry. After the burning of the store and the destruction of the hotel there had been no food available in Coxville. He wondered if John's shrewd brain had figured this out, and if the thought had prompted the burning of the place. Certainly it meant that neither he nor the girl could stay too long hidden in the hills. He dared not try his hand at hunting since the sound of a gun would only bring the searchers to their hiding place.

He watched, and the girl slept, curled up on the blanket in the warm sun. At about 10:00 in the morning he saw a rider come down the trail from the pass and judged that this would be the man who John had left behind to wait for their escape.

It was too far for him to recognize the rider, or the other two who came down from the hills on the right to join him in the bottom of the valley.

They stopped, holding an extensive conference, and were joined by two other men, coming from the direction of the main ranch.

He judged that he was perhaps seven crow-flight miles from the ranch buildings, but it would be twice, perhaps three times as far by trail because of the broken nature of the country between.

It was a country of small sharp valleys, of steep hills with patches of timber on the minor crests, a country where a smart man could elude pursuers for days if they did not find his tracks.

Ray had very little real fear of discovery as long as he and Marty remained where they were. The horses had been carefully hidden so that they could not be spotted from any of the surrounding hills, and their own concealment was excellent.

But if they should venture into the open, they would be seen immediately. All during the slow afternoon hours he witnessed the pattern of search unfold below him. John seemed to be using the full crew, and for all its apparent aimlessness it was a careful hunt. They were quartering the ground in pairs, working each small valley as if combing the rough land for stray beef at roundup, searching the ridges and the timber that crowned them, and always working farther and farther eastward.

He saw them appear and disappear. At times all the hunters would be screened from his sight for a full half hour; at others ten or twelve would be in view, keeping contact with each other as they drifted forward.

It would only be a matter of time until they reached this side of the valley and began to comb the small hills directly below him. He looked up, measuring the distance of the sun above the western horizon.

It was, he knew, a race between the searching men and time, for if he and the girl were forced to shift their hiding place before full dark, they were bound to be spotted. The shadows lengthened, the sun swung low toward the western mountains. The searchers were still moving nearer. He heard a sound behind him and turned his head to find Marty at his elbow.

She said in a reproachful voice: "You let me sleep all day. You should have wakened me. You should have let me stand my share of the watch."

"I had some rest," he lied.

"What's happened?"

For answer he pointed to the moving figures, still distinguishable in the gathering darkness. "They've been working toward us all day. Another half hour of light and we'd have been forced to move."

She considered the figures below her. "Will they continue the search after dark?"

He shrugged. "Maybe, after the moon comes up. But there will be a couple of useless hours between sunset and moonrise. My guess is, they'll build a fire and cook some supper."

"I wish they'd invite us," Marty said. "I'm starved."

So was Ray. His stomach felt as if it had always been empty. He said: "If I'm right, we'll wait until they light the fire and we have them spotted. Then we'll try slipping past them toward the ranch."

She gave a startled gasp. "You're going to the Box D?"

"It's the closest place to get anything to eat," he told her, "and, besides, I think we should have a copy of that will."

"There's a copy at the lawyer's office in Dondaro. I heard him warn John. I think John was getting ready to destroy it. The will, I mean."

"I thought the lawyer was on John's side."

"He's a scared little man, Ray. He'd help

John as long as he thought it was safe, but I don't think he'd destroy his copy of the will. He'd be afraid that Aunt Kate might recover sufficiently to find out what he'd done."

"Anyway," Ray said, "we'll try to slip through to the ranch. With most of the crew out hunting us here, it will be about as safe a place as we can go. We can also find out how your aunt is, and it's shorter to town by the ranch than it would be twisting our way through the hills."

"What do you plan to do, Ray?" Her tone said that it was his decision, that she would follow along no matter what he suggested.

He shook his head. "I don't quite know." This wasn't the exact truth, but he saw no point in worrying her more than need be.

They waited. The valley shrouded with the night until they lost the moving searchers in the gloom. Finally a fire blossomed on the valley floor. Ray lifted himself to his feet.

"Now's the time to move, and move fast. They'll all ride in at the first chance for food. Half an hour from now some of them may be drifting again."

She followed without words as he led the way down the steep slope to where he had staked the horses and hastily threw the saddles on the rested animals.

Before he stepped up into his own saddle,

he told her tensely: "If they spot us, break directly for the ranch. I'll lead them west and try to lose them in the hills, but don't ride up to the house until you see me come in. If I don't show, pull out for town and try to get away on the stage."

She did not answer. Marty Donovan had enough of Kate's spirit in her so that she would never consciously run from any fight. If they were chased, she had no intention of deserting Ray. She'd stay with him to the end. Either they'd come up to the ranch together, or neither of them would ever get there.

The fire was a winking eye off to the right, flickering in the little gusts of wind that swept through the wide throat of the valley.

Their horses walked carefully as if they sensed that they, too, were among the hunted, that a chance misstep would bring the Box D crew thundering after them.

Ray swung around the shoulder of the ridge. He knew that the searching men would find their tracks in the morning light. He had to expect that, but daylight was a good ten hours away.

The ridge finally hid the fire and he circled on, hunting through the darkness for the trail that would lead downward to the ranch buildings.

251

The going was slow, the land very rough. Twice he got down and led the horse, feeling as if by instinct the way across the rocks.

By the time they reached the trail, the moon was a yellow half circle in the sky and he turned his horse into the beaten track with a distinct feeling of relief. The worst was over, at least for the moment, and he shook out the reins, letting the impatient horse run.

The bunkhouse lay in darkness when they pulled up to the edge of the corral. There was a light in the cook shack and another in the main house.

He stepped down, whispering to the girl to hold his horse, then slipped across the rough ground, his gun in his hand. He was too old a campaigner not to make certain of his retreat, and he stepped carefully through the bunkhouse door, pausing in the stuffy darkness, still warm from the heat of the day.

He stood perfectly still, listening, trying by instinctive sense to determine whether there was anyone within the silent building.

Finally he risked the flare of a match. The main room was deserted, but two of the doors to the bunk rooms were closed. He crossed to the first, still holding the match, and eased the door inward.

The tight hinges creaked. He stopped, listening for any stir from within. He heard none. He dropped the match as it burned his fingers and slipped into the room. The bunks were empty. That might mean the full crew was out in the hills, still searching for him and the girl. He was moving toward the doorway when the cook suddenly appeared in the entrance, carrying a lighted lantern.

The man's eyes widened. He started to back out. Ray brought the gun up. "Hold it," he said.

Instead of obeying, the cook swung the lantern, hurling it directly at Ray's head. Then he ducked back around the protection of the doorjamb.

Ray jumped sidewise more by instinct than by plan and the lantern struck his shoulder, bounded off, and landed on the table. By a miracle it went out without breaking.

He threw only a quick glance in its direction to make certain that it would not fire the bunkhouse, then went after the cook. It would have been easy to shoot down the fleeing man, but he did not want to alarm anyone who might be in the big house.

The cook was fat, and he wasn't used to running, and apparently he had no gun. He started for the cook shack, and then, as if realizing that it offered poor shelter, he switched direction and scuttled for the main house.

Ray caught him just short of the porch, bringing him down with a flying tackle, his big body pinning the struggling man to the ground.

"Behave, or I'll beat your brains out," Ray said.

The cook was very scared. "Don't hit me." He had a crooked arm up to protect his face. "Don't hit me."

Ray climbed to his feet. "Get up."

The man rose slowly.

"Who's in the house?"

"Juanita."

"And Aunt Kate?"

"She died, just before dark."

Ray tried to believe that. Then: "You mean that John took all the men with him to the hills?"

"All but The Kid. Juanita sent him out to find John as soon as the old lady died."

Ray studied the man's face and decided that he was telling the truth. "All right. Walk over to the storeroom and no tricks."

"But. . . ."

"March."

The cook marched. After Ray had locked

254

the man in the room that had served as his own prison, he whistled for Marty. The girl rode toward him through the growing moonlight, leading his horse.

He helped her from the saddle, saying in an undertone: "Aunt Kate died at sundown."

She was perfectly motionless for a long moment, then she said in a strained voice: "She died alone. She raised three . . . no, four of us . . . and she died alone."

He didn't answer. There did not seem to be anything much to say. It sounded the perfect epitaph for Kate Donovan's life. She had been a lonely person, and, although she had raised four children who were not her own, she had given her love to only one of them, and even that love had taken the form of bullying Bert until he ran away.

No, he thought, she had died as she had lived, lonely and self-centered. The ranch had been her only real interest, and now her two remaining heirs were struggling for possession of the ranch.

"We'll have to move fast," he said. "The cook said that Juanita sent The Kid after John as soon as Aunt Kate died. We must have passed him on the trail, coming in."

"But we didn't see anyone."

"True enough. The Kid probably heard us

coming and pulled off into the brush to see who it was. I should have been more careful, but it never occurred to me that anyone would be coming out from the ranch. Anyway, the harm's done. We haven't too much time now."

He led the way into the house. They had barely appeared in the central hall when Juanita came out of Aunt Kate's room. She was a large Mexican woman, squat and almost as broad as she was tall.

Juanita dissolved into tears and gathered Marty into her arms. "Honey, she's dead. She's dead."

Marty tried to comfort the woman who had spent most of her adult life in caring for that house. Ray left them in the hall, went into the big front room, and crossed to the old-fashioned desk. The tin box stood on its little shelf as it had stood all during his childhood. He picked it up, noting that it was locked, and wasted no time. The hunting knife that Aunt Kate had used as a letter opener lay on the desk. He slid the broad blade under the edge of the box's lip and pried. The lock snapped and the box came open.

It was nearly full: old receipts, tally sheets, shares in the local bank, and the will. He unfolded the form, read the contents quickly, then slid it into his pocket and returned to the hall. Marty was just coming out of Aunt Kate's room, her arm about the broad shoulders of the Mexican woman.

"That's enough," she told Juanita. "You know she wouldn't want you to cry. She didn't believe in tears."

The words only increased the sobbing and Marty looked at Ray helplessly. She was very white and her gray eyes showed a deep hurt. The passing of Kate Donovan had come as a hard shock.

Ray said gently: "Time to ride."

Juanita's head bobbed up quickly. "Take me with you. I don't want to stay here now. I'm afraid. I'm afraid of John."

"We'll be back," Ray said. "Just tell John that. We'll be back." There was no time to argue. If he meant to get to Dondaro ahead of John, they must ride now.

XIII

Kandee left Peggy Squires's house by the rear door a good two hours after dark and walked along the wide street, keeping in the shadows. In a town the size of Dondaro it was almost impossible for anyone to remain in hiding long. There simply weren't enough places of concealment.

It galled Kandee that he had been forced to remain out of sight. It was not that he feared a personal meeting with Sam Friend or with any of Wilbur Keats's men, but he realized that after the proposition they had made him in connection with Bert's murder, they could not knowingly let him remain in town and live. And he meant to live, to live at least long enough to see the outcome of the Donovan business. For almost a year, in his mind, he had associated himself with the Donovans — or rather with Marty Donovan. He had watched her ride the streets of Dondaro, proud and young and free.

He was not free, and he knew that he would never be free again. As if to remind himself, he coughed heavily and was forced to lean against the corner of a building, white-faced and gasping.

No, he wasn't free. Death had its fingers upon him. He did not fear death but he did not want to die until this girl who he had come to love was safe.

Peggy Squires's house not only offered him a sanctuary, but also a source of news. The men who came to visit Peggy's girls told of the happenings of the town and the countryside. From this gossip Kandee had learned that Bert Donovan was dead. He felt no sorrow about Bert Donovan. With his experienced eye he had marked the younger nephew of the Box D owner as a pleasant weakling, a man who made a good companion at the poker table or at the bar, but one not strong enough to hold the ranch or to protect Martha.

It was Ray Donovan who interested Kandee. He heard with foreboding that Ray had been held a prisoner at the ranch after Bert's murder, and that Ray had escaped. He even heard about the attack on Coxville and Dupont's death and the burning of the store and old hotel. One of the Box D riders had come in that morning for cartridges and he knew that both Ray Donovan and Martha were loose, somewhere in the hills.

Nor did he need to be told that Dondaro was seething with excitement. The town drew a good part of its life from the Box D, and it was important to the merchants to know who would have control, now that the old lady was paralyzed. They gathered in groups at the street corners and in the saloons, discussing it.

Kandee crossed the street to avoid one such group. He walked aimlessly, yet his steps carried him toward the livery stable. He had not as yet made up his mind, but he was considering riding into the hills in search of Ray and the girl. And then he saw them in the half light from the distant moon. He knew at once who they were, although he lacked a clear view of their faces.

They came along the alley, cautiously. He waited until they came abreast of the barn's rear door before he moved out of his screening shadows.

"Donovan."

Ray reacted out of sheer instinct. His hand swept down to his holstered gun and it seemed to leap up to meet his curving fingers as he swung in the saddle to face the gambler.

"What are you doing here?"

Kandee's low laugh with its edge of hidden mockery reached him. "Waiting for you, my friend."

Donovan grunted. Kandee had puzzled him from the first. The man's attitude of seeming friendship made little or no sense.

"How'd you know we were going to ride in?" His tone was full of suspicion. Behind him Marty sat motionlessly, her hand on the gun at her side.

"I didn't." The mockery had faded from Kandee's tone. "But I heard that you were out in the hills and that the Box D crew was hunting you."

"They still are."

The gambler took no notice. "And I walked down here, debating whether I should get a horse and ride out in an attempt to find you."

"Why should you?"

For an instant Kandee's eyes wavered to the girl. She was watching him, puzzled, and he knew a momentary regret that she would probably never know, never understand. Then he moved his thin shoulders in the tiniest of shrugs. What difference did it make, he thought. Better this way. If the cards of life had fallen in another pattern he might have told her, but they hadn't so fallen, and he was gambler enough to accept the deal that fate had dealt him. It was enough to know that he was present at a time when she had need, and that he could help to meet that need.

"I told you once," he said, speaking to Donovan, "that I chose to help you. What matter the reason? For believe me, my friend, both you and the little lady need whatever help you can get, and you are in no position to be particular about the source."

Ray Donovan knew he was right.

"And the worst place you could have come to is Dondaro. John Donovan controls this town, and with his aunt paralyzed his

261

word will very nearly be law."

"His aunt is dead," Donovan said, and swung from the saddle. "And we had to come. Her will leaves the ranch to Marty."

Kandee touched his hat to the girl. "My congratulations," he said, and mockery was back in his tone.

"Thank you." Marty's words told nothing of her inner feelings. At the instant she was as good at masking her emotions as either Ray or Kandee.

Kandee's smile never wavered. "I am afraid you may have some difficulty in achieving your inheritance. You have Mister Tough Donovan to help you, and no doubt his help is worth an army. But still, your cousin John is the big man in town."

Ray Donovan said shortly: "She'll probably have more difficulty than you realize. She doesn't get the ranch until she marries."

Kandee looked at the girl, then at Donovan. "I don't see why that should be such a difficulty."

"Don't you?" It was Donovan's turn to be sarcastic. "Perhaps you even have a suggestion as to whom she might marry since you seem to know so much about our affairs."

The gambler was smiling now. "That's the simplest question I've had to answer in thirty-five years. You. You're the most convenient. She knows and trusts you. And you are perfectly able to fight for her rights. A lot of people who might stand against her otherwise will hesitate to go up against you."

Ray Donovan was too startled to speak. He had been conditioned to think of Martha only in connection with Bert. The idea that he might have a valid chance to marry her had not even entered his mind.

He started to turn to the girl, but she answered even before he could frame the question.

"Why not? Mister Kandee seems to be smarter than either of us."

Her tone showed no emotion, as if she were merely being practical. Here was a situation that she had to meet, and she was meeting it with the same calm that Kate Donovan might have exhibited in a similar situation. For an instant he felt an uncontrollable sting of dismay at what might be regarded by Marty as a marriage of convenience. He wanted Marty, but he wanted her whole love as well.

Ray knew that she liked him, trusted him, even honored him — but suddenly he wished that her feelings went deeper. He had given very little thought to marriage. He had known very few women intimately enough to speculate much about it. How would it feel to be married to Martha?

To cover what threatened to be an awkward pause he said: "It's all very well to talk of marrying, but not as simple as it might be. As you said, Dondaro is pretty well under John Donovan's control, and John and his friends would go to almost any lengths to see that Marty doesn't marry . . . at least, anyone except John."

The girl said quickly: "But there must be some way . . . some place where we would be safe, where the ceremony could be performed without John's friends knowing that we were in town." She appealed to Kandee. "You know the town better than we do. Perhaps you have a friend . . . ?"

For the first time since Ray had known him the gambler seemed embarrassed. He opened his mouth twice before any sound came out, and then he said slowly: "I am not very popular in Dondaro, Miss Donovan. In fact, I've been in hiding for several days."

"But where were you hiding?"

Color came up to make a crimson blotch on each of Kandee's thin white cheeks. "I'm afraid that would hardly be a satisfactory place, although I will say nothing against her since she protected and cared for me when I needed help. I'm speaking of Peggy Squires."

Ray Donovan started at the name. In a town the size of Dondaro it was impossible to conceal anyone's occupation, and Peggy Squires had operated her house for nearly a dozen years.

He was about to agree with Kandee, but as before Martha Donovan gave him no chance to answer.

She said: "If Miss Squires will let us use her parlor for a little while, I think we should both be very grateful."

Kandee started to protest, but Martha Donovan cut him short. There was a new dignity about her, striking in one so young.

"You are," she told Kandee, "a gambler. And at times a gambler is not rated much higher than Peggy Squires."

Kandee's face was very red now, and Ray Donovan wondered if he finally would explode with anger. But Marty stepped forward and laid her hand on the gambler's arm.

"I did not say that to criticize," she told him. "I hadn't finished. You are a professional gambler, yet you are the only person in this town . . . the town that I have a right to consider as home . . . who has offered Ray and me your help. We're pleased and proud to have it, and we'd be as pleased and proud to have help from Peggy Squires if it were offered as honestly."

Kandee bowed. There was something of old world grace in the gesture, something learned in a softer, more formalized society.

"I ask pardon," he murmured. "I should have known that anyone so beautiful could not help being gracious. Will you follow me now?"

XIV

Kandee left Donovan and Martha in the shadows at the rear of the house and slipped quietly through the kitchen door. Alone with Martha, he tried to utter a final protest, but she stopped him with a finger against his lips.

Inside, Kandee moved along the hall and into the small, private sitting room that Peggy maintained as her own. She looked up now and there was a trace of annoyance in her dark eyes. "You've been out. You're a fool. If Sam Friend sees you, you're a dead man. I wish to the devil you'd let me sneak you out of town."

He coughed and was forced to await the return of his breath before he could speak. When he recovered, he said: "Perhaps after tonight it won't be necessary for me to run."

At once her suspicion flared. "What fool thing are you planning now? You're not going after Sam Friend? You'll merely get yourself killed."

He waved a slender hand. "Thanks for your concern, Peggy." There was no mockery in his voice now; it betrayed genuine emotion. "You've been the best friend I could have had. But I have one small remaining favor to ask. Two friends of mine wish to be married. They have no place to go, and it's important that Wilbur Keats and his men do not know they're in town. Could they use this room?"

She peered at him as if she were certain that he had taken leave of his senses. "Are you crazy?"

His smile was warm but somber. "I have done many silly things in my miserable life," he told her. "But I assure you that this is not one of them."

"But. . . ."

He stopped her with a gesture. "Please, Peggy, hear me out." He went on to explain that Kate Donovan was dead, that John was trying to take the ranch from the girl, and that Martha could not come into her inheritance until she married. "Cupid is a rather strange rôle for me to be playing," he added.

"Almost as strange as your running a wedding. But life sometimes casts us in strange rôles."

Peggy Squires's bluntness matched her shrewd insight. She said flatly: "What's this girl mean to you, Kandee?"

Kandee got out a twisted smile. "Why nothing, Peggy. And yet, everything. I've watched her ride, wild and free, along the streets, a princess, yet kind, with a good word for everyone. She represents to me what could have been and never was."

Peggy Squires fingered an earring and frowned. "She'd never come here."

"There you're wrong." He was on surer ground now. "She's in the alley, waiting only for your permission to come in. I suggested that it was not a proper place and she put me to shame with her honesty and lack of pretense. Only the small people of the earth are bound by conventions and intolerance. The big people, the people of truly great heart, are not affected by the petty judgments of others."

Peggy Squires appreciated the eloquence in this man. Kandee, she thought, might have been a great orator in other circumstances. He had an inner power, when he chose to exert it, that beat down the objections brought against him. She realized that what he asked might involve her in deep trouble. If John Donovan or Wilbur Keats learned that she had helped Martha and Ray Donovan, her days here were numbered. She made her decision and rose.

"Bring them in," she said.

It was Peggy Squires who was embarrassed by the meeting. Marty seemed as calm and natural as if this woman with her painted cheeks had not been discussed for years in whispers by the children of the town.

She thanked Peggy courteously and waited in silence while Ray Donovan and Kandee argued as to who should go after the judge. The gambler won by the simple expedient of walking out of the house.

Ray hesitated, hating to leave Martha there alone, and by the time he reached the rear door Kandee had gone far up the street.

Peggy Squires gave her girls orders to lock the front door and to admit no one. She was afraid that one of Wilbur Keats's men would come in, realize that something out of the ordinary was happening, and bring his boss or Sam Friend to investigate.

She feared Keats although she had a working agreement with him. It would have been impossible for her to operate without such an agreement.

But she was no more worried than Kandee. He moved along the dark alley as quietly as possible. Now more than ever he did not want to run into Sam Friend.

The showdown that he knew had to come eventually must be delayed until after the wedding. Ever since Ray Donovan had returned to Dondaro, he had felt that Martha's only chance of standing against her cousin John lay in Ray Donovan. For himself he realized that he was too sick to be of much help to her for long. But once she and Ray were married, he was certain that Donovan would find a way to stand against those who opposed her. He had the greatest confidence in Donovan and his ability to handle any situation that might arise.

He had to cross the main street to reach the judge's house, and he watched for his chance, standing in the alley mouth, waiting until the block on either side was almost clear.

Then he walked across, because a running man would attract attention. He walked hunched over a little so that anyone seeing him from a distance would not recognize his tall figure. He did not breathe easily until he reached the far alley mouth and disappeared into its shadowy depths.

Judge Austin B. Parkman was a small man

of nearly sixty. He lived in a square, clapboard house of which he was very proud. In fact, he was a rather proud man, self-satisfied and quite certain that he was one of Dondaro's more prominent citizens. His feeling, however, was shared by few other people.

He sat at his desk now, under the cone of light from the green-shaded student lamp working on his history of the law in the early mining camps. He had been working on it for twenty years and would work on it until the day he died. Even he realized that it probably would never be published.

He heard a slight noise behind him and sat very still. He lived alone, a part-time housekeeper coming in to do for him three days each week.

At last he turned to find Kandee's tall form, blocking the doorway. This discomfited him more than ever, since he knew, as did most of the citizens of Dondaro, that Wilbur Keats's men had been searching for the gambler for several days.

"What do you want?" The judge's busy mind frisked back through the past to recall any occasion when he might have offended this gambler.

Kandee read the fear in the judge's eyes. His respect for Parkman was not great. He knew that before Wilbur Keats had rigged his election as judge, Parkman had been a small-town lawyer with a paltry practice.

"Couple of friends of mine want to get married," Kandee said. "Get your hat and come on."

Parkman did not move. His round, rather moon-like face showed nothing but surprise. "Want to get married? Have them come here."

"They can't," Kandee said.

"Where are they?" Parkman's interest grew.

"At Peggy Squires's."

The judge started to chuckle. "That's a strange place for a wedding."

Kandee did not change expression. "Know of a better one?"

"Well," — the judge slapped his leg — "now that you mention it, I can't say as I do."

He rose and got his hat from the tree in the corner. "Wait until I tell the boys downtown. Haven't heard of anything so funny in years. Do I know the groom?"

"You probably haven't seen him in a long time." Kandee was being carefully non-committal. There was a good chance still that he would not get the judge back to Peggy's without meeting Sam Friend, in which case he felt that the less Parkman knew the better.

The judge started toward the front door, but Kandee stopped him. "If it's all the same to you, we'll use the alley."

Parkman nodded, looking at his companion curiously. He had never known Kandee well, but the man had always puzzled him. The gambler was so obviously well-bred that Parkman found it difficult to place the man in his proper category. He guessed that Kandee was a member of some good family who had gotten in trouble and headed West. From the soft overtones of the man's speech he surmised that Kandee's former home had been somewhere in the South.

Parkman did not know why Wilbur Keats was hunting for the gambler, and he did not much care. While he owed his place as judge to Keats, he was not a close member of the man's gang and he knew nothing about Friend's offer to Kandee in regard to Bert Donovan's death.

They moved along the alley through the shadows, not speaking. Parkman had his own ideas about the coming wedding. He had decided that Kandee himself was marrying one of Peggy Squires's girls and did not want the town in general to know.

It was, he thought, too good a joke to

spoil. In the ordinary course of events he would have tried in some way to let Sam Friend or Wilbur Keats know that the gambler was still in town, but with the prospect of the wedding he was almost as anxious to avoid them as was Kandee himself.

They reached the main street and paused until the walk on either side was clear of casual loiterers. Then they walked quickly across through the deep dust.

Once again in the shadows of the alley, the gambler relaxed a little. He had been tense crossing the street, lighted as it was by the lamps in the store windows. They reached Peggy Squires's house. He held the rear door open for the judge, then followed him down the hallway into Peggy's room.

Parkman saw Martha Donovan and his round face went crimson.

"Whose idea of a joke is this?"

Ray Donovan took a quick step forward, but Kandee motioned him back with a small wave of his thin hand. His whole attention was on the judge, his deep-set eyes dark and burning as if lighted by the fever that wracked his slender body.

"Your Honor," he said, "there are times when gentlemen contain their anger, especially in the presence of a lady."

Some of the red faded from Judge Parkman's face, leaving it white and curiously drawn.

He tried to speak twice before he could control his voice sufficiently to say: "I refuse to be a party to any of this." He looked at Martha. "I don't know what coercion these men have employed to force you into this peculiar situation, Miss Donovan, but I want you to understand that I'm not part of their plans."

Martha Donovan was the most self-contained person in the room. "I think you are laboring under a misapprehension, Judge. Ray and I want to be married, and it so happens that there are people in Dondaro who might want to prevent our marriage. Miss Squires has kindly loaned us her house and Mister Kandee kindly went to fetch you. Other than that, neither of them has anything to do with it."

Parkman glanced from one to the other. He had already talked with John Donovan's lawyer about Kate's will, and he was perfectly familiar with the marriage clause that the will contained. He also knew that, if he performed this ceremony, John Donovan and therefore Wilbur Keats would never forgive him.

He scrutinized Ray Donovan, noting how

big he was, noting the straight, square jaw, remembering the stories about this man. For a moment he thought that perhaps John Donovan had met his match, then he remembered that Wilbur Keats was allied with John, and that they had available not only Keats's men but also the full Box D crew.

He said to the girl: "I think you're making a great mistake. Your cousin John will no doubt look after your interests, while this man . . ." — he indicated Ray with a motion of his hand — "I understand that he's wanted for questioning with regard to your other cousin's death."

Martha stepped forward. "Judge Parkman," she said, "I'm perfectly capable of taking care of my own affairs. In years past my aunt ran her ranch, and for that matter ran this part of the country. She rode out with her crew then, and she handled a gun herself. I realize that you feel indebted to Wilbur Keats. I know you also believe that John will take my aunt's place. I'm here to tell you now that you're wrong. The Box D is mine. I intend to run the ranch as I choose, and those who get in my way will regret it. Now, please proceed with the ceremony."

Parkman caught his breath in unwilling admiration. This slip of a girl looked and acted like Kate Donovan.

In that moment he made his choice. It wasn't the guns that showed plainly at Ray Donovan's hips, nor the gun that he knew was hidden in the shoulder holster beneath Kandee's coat. It was the girl. He felt that he was facing another Kate Donovan, a woman strong enough to dominate the whole country.

He cleared his throat nervously. "Shall we begin?"

Peggy Squires had not uttered a word since the judge entered the room, but now she said hesitantly: "I . . . I'd like to ask a favor." She glanced at Martha.

The girl smiled. "I don't think you need to ask any favors, Missus Squires. After all, this is your place."

The woman's face showed red under her paint. "It's just that the girls would like to come in. They never saw a wedding, most of them, and they're not likely to see another."

Kandee took half a step forward as if to protest, but Martha gave him no chance. "Of course," she said. "Both Ray and I would be honored."

Peggy Squires disappeared into the hall. There were excited whisperings from the next room, and then she returned, followed

277

by the four girls walking in single file. They lined up against the wall, keeping their eyes averted so that they did not meet Martha's gaze.

But this did not stop her from saying: "It's nice of you to serve as our witnesses. I want to thank each one of you."

Kandee watched it all with the air of a detached spectator. He thought that this probably was the strangest wedding anyone had ever seen. Ordinarily it would have appealed to his sense of humor, for in sheer self-defense he had wrapped himself in a robe of cynicism. But he was not feeling cynical at the moment.

Nor was he the only one who was affected by the ceremony. He watched Ray and noted the grave way in which Donovan answered the judge's questions, the serious unsmiling glance that he turned to the girl at his side. Ray Donovan, no matter what reason he had for marrying this girl, was not taking the union lightly.

The judge was deadly serious, also, as if he realized that he had taken an irrevocable step, aligning himself with the forces that were preparing to battle his friends for this corner of the land. He did not hurry the service. He pronounced each word clearly,

distinctly, so no one could fail to understand.

Peggy Squires cried openly, dabbing at her
eyes with the bit of lace that served as her
handkerchief. The four girls stared at the
rug, never changing expression.

And then, just as the judge said — "By
the authority vested in me by the territorial
government, I now pronounce you man and
wife." — the knock sounded at the front
door.

Everyone started. Kandee took a half step,
but Peggy was before him, ducking into the
hall, saying softly: "I'll get rid of them."

They heard her open the door. They heard
her slam and lock it. Then she rushed back
into the room, her face white. "It's the Box
D," she whispered. "They're searching the
town."

XV

John Donovan pulled into the ranch yard
ahead of the Box D crew. He stepped from
the saddle, calling the cook's name as he
moved toward the bunkhouse. He was
answered by a pounding from inside the
storeroom. Reaching the fastened door, he
pulled the bar from the staples and let the
cook out.

"Where are they?"

The cook blinked at him in the half light from the moon. "I heard them ride out. They went to the house first."

Without a word John swung on his boot heel and ran toward the big house. Juanita met him in the hall. She was still crying. John brushed by her and strode into the big room.

The tin box lay open where Ray had left it. John stopped, staring down at it with eyes that had suddenly gained a crazed glare. He had always hated Ray Donovan. Throughout his childhood he had looked upon Ray as an interloper, a nameless nobody who by his personality held the regard of both Bert and Marty.

John had been jealous even then. There was a drive within him that craved the respect and liking of the people around him. It had nothing to do with his personal feelings for these people. He felt little but contempt for them, but his egomaniacal desire was to be looked up to and revered by all.

And he blamed his own personal shortcomings on the boy who outshone him in everything that he tried to accomplish.

And now, just when his careful planning of years was about to bear fruit, this same

Ray Donovan rose up again to block him. He had never doubted his ability to control Marty. Marty would come to heel because of sheer necessity. Without Ray she could not possibly stand against him, against the power he had built up for himself. But now she had Ray Donovan, and Ray Donovan had the will.

He judged Ray's motives by his own — Ray wanted the ranch. He could figure it no other way. Ray was a bully boy, a hired gunman, employed by the railroads to control the riff-raff in the railhead towns, a bucko no better than the laborers he controlled. Ray would jump at the chance to get the ranch. Who wouldn't? But Ray was never going to have the Box D.

John Donovan was not a man who often gave way to his emotions, but he gave way to his hate now. Juanita had been watching him from the doorway through red-rimmed eyes. As he turned to leave, she threw a dozen questions in his direction, but it was as if he did not hear.

He pushed her out of his way once more. He stamped through the front door and across the baked surface of the yard to where the crew waited, still lounging in the saddles.

"They were here," he said. "They've

headed for town. We're going after them and we're going to get him. A thousand dollars gold to the man who finds Ray Donovan and stops him. Let's ride."

They rode. Most of this crew had little feeling for the ranch. Most of them had no love for John. They were hard, cynical, and uncaring, but they recognized the tough core within him and it won their unwilling admiration. To them he was power. He represented the ranch, one of the largest ranches in the country. He paid well, and would continue to pay. They rode hard, driving their horses as if each one bore a personal malice toward the man they hunted.

They came into Dondaro, sliding their horses up to the rail before the livery, and scattering, searching the saloons as they moved along the main street, questioning the bartenders, the card players, the loafers.

John went directly to Wilbur Keats's office. He found Sam Friend in the chair beside the battered desk, talking to Keats. Friend watched Donovan with full attention, a small smile on his thin lips, his light eyes telling nothing of his thoughts.

Keats shook his head at John Donovan's question. "They haven't come into town. That I'm certain of. One of the boys would have let me know the minute they were spotted."

John said stubbornly: "They have to be here somewhere. They wouldn't run out . . . that much I'm sure of. They'll have to probate that will in Parkman's court. Get hold of Parkman. Tell him I want him to stall it. I don't care what he tells them. He can say that because Marty isn't married the court will administer the estate until she is, and have me appointed administrator."

"You shouldn't have let them get hold of that will," Keats said. "You should have destroyed it."

John snorted at him. "Are you crazy? I didn't dare before Kate died. If she had rallied and found out what I'd done, the fat would really have been in the fire."

"I don't like it," Keats grumbled. "I've played your game for three years, John, and I've seen precious little return for my trouble. I started this railroad company. I applied for the charter because you thought it would scare Kate so badly that she'd turn her affairs over to you. It didn't work. It was a fool idea from the start."

John Donovan took one step and grasped the collar of Keats's coat. He hoisted Keats to his feet and jerked him forward until their faces were only inches apart.

"I made you," he said. "I took you out from behind a bar and made you, and, if it serves my purpose, I'll unmake you. What's the matter . . . afraid of Ray?"

Sam Friend slid back his chair and came to his feet.

"Let him go, Donovan."

John twisted to look at Friend. He said: "I have no time for two-bit killers. Crawl into your hole." He shoved Keats back into his chair and wiped his mouth with the back of his hand.

Afterward, as if he had gotten a checkrein upon his feelings, he said in a level tone: "We're all upset. Let's not quit now. We've got things almost in our grasp."

He studied them as if he had never seen them before. Then without further words he swung on his heel and left the office. Sam Friend had not moved. Sam said in a flat tone: "Looks like your partner is coming apart at the seams."

Without waiting for an answer he moved off into the night.

He stopped in the shadow of one of the roof awnings and watched John Donovan giving orders to his men. They separated into groups of three and started up the side streets, pausing to knock at every door.

It was The Kid who mounted the steps of

Peggy Squires's house. Baldy called to him from the board sidewalk: "They won't be in there, you fool."

The Kid paid no attention. He knocked heavily on the door. After a minute's wait, the door opened and Baldy had a glimpse of Peggy Squires. He heard The Kid's mumbled question and saw the woman slam the door. Then he doubled over in quick, shaking laughter.

"First man ever got thrown out of there," he said between chuckles. "Wait'll I tell the boys."

The Kid did not think it was funny. He started to kick the door down.

Inside, the people in Peggy Squires's sitting room winced expectantly. Ray Donovan started for the hall. Kandee caught his arm.

"Get her out the back way. Let me handle this."

Donovan hesitated. Never in his life had he run out and let someone else carry his fight. It was contrary to every instinct of his nature.

"You take her out. This is my battle."

"You fool." Kandee let his voice rise. "Don't you understand? It's you they're looking for. If they find you here, what will they do to Peggy and her girls?"

Peggy swore under her breath. From behind the chair in the corner she brought out an old double-barreled shotgun. "It'll take more than John Donovan and his Box D crowd to do anything to me," she said.

Ray hesitated. Marty had his arm. "Let's get out of here," she said. "We'll only make it worse for them."

Parkman headed for the rear door. Ray went after him. He didn't trust the judge. Parkman made the alley first and started to run. Ray caught him before he reached the corner of the main street. Marty came up a moment later, her gun in her hand.

Behind them, The Kid had finally succeeded in kicking down the door. He started into the hallway of Peggy's house and stopped. Kandee had stepped from the small sitting room and was standing, facing him. Kandee didn't say anything, but something in his manner scared The Kid. The Kid's hand streaked toward his belted gun.

But he never touched it. Kandee shot him twice. The gambler was as quiet and unhurried as if he had been sitting behind a table, dealing cards, and quite as dispassionate. He had no feeling about The Kid, one way or the other. The Kid had come into this hallway through a broken door, ready to kill. Kandee had stopped him.

Baldy had been standing on the sidewalk, still laughing, and the blast of Kandee's first shot cut the laugh in the middle. Motionless, he saw The Kid stagger back out of the doorway and collapse on the porch. With a roar that would have done credit to a range bull he ripped the gun from his holster and charged up the steps. The second Box D man had been twenty feet away. He ran up, shouting, pulling his gun as he came.

"What happened, Baldy? What happened?"

Baldy didn't answer. He jumped into the doorway, saw Kandee, and raised his gun. His trigger squeeze was interrupted by the brazen bellow of Peggy Squires's twin-barreled shotgun. The heavy shot pattern tore his chest apart and knocked him flat. The man on the porch turned and ran down the street, yelling at the top of his voice. Ten minutes later the full Box D crew converged upon Peggy Squires's house. Aside from the two dead men on the porch they found it empty.

XVI

Wilbur Keats sat alone in his office. He had heard the shots and the shouting as the Box D crew assembled, but he had not stirred.

Like most of the townsmen he knew what was going on, and was very careful to keep clear of it. The street outside his office looked deserted. It would stay deserted until the Box D found Ray Donovan or rode out.

Wilbur Keats was trying to think. He had not liked John Donovan's words or manner. When he had first begun to play Donovan's game, he had thought that after the final showdown he, not Donovan, might well be in control. He had not rated Donovan very highly, either for nerve or brains.

But tonight he had seen a new John Donovan, one who he had not guessed existed. This man who had first listened to advice when Keats offered it was now taking command. And Keats was not at all certain in his own mind where his position in John Donovan's scheme of things would be.

He heard a noise at the door behind him. He turned, expecting Sam Friend with a report on the street's happenings. It wasn't Friend. Ray Donovan stood there, completely filling the doorway.

Donovan crossed the room and pulled down the window blind.

Keats reacted with unwonted slowness. His mind had been on other things and it took a full moment to bring it into focus.

Then he said quietly: "You know they're

searching the town for you."

Donovan nodded. He showed no concern, but he did steal a quick look at the street outside through the crack beside the blind. Wilbur Keats watched him. Suddenly he realized that he had never met a man like this one. There was an implacable quality about Ray Donovan, a calm, careful, plodding deadliness.

Keats had known many gunmen. They all had emotional weaknesses, nervous lapses, and always in the end these flaws killed them.

But Donovan showed no emotion whatever. He was a man doing a job, doing it thoroughly, never stopping to consider what it might cost him. He was as unstoppable as a landslide, as irrepressible as a swelling flood. It was the quality in him that the toughs of the railroad towns had sensed, and not understood, and feared. Suddenly Wilbur Keats was afraid.

Nearly twenty men roamed the dark streets without, hunting this intruder, and yet at the moment, deep within his heart, Keats knew that Donovan could not and would not be stopped. Some of this feeling was in his voice, making it shake a little when he said: "It's not my men hunting you." He said it in defense, as if he were trying to establish an alibi for what was to happen.

"Isn't it?" Donovan said. He was still unhurried. "You have a railroad company formed and you hold a charter from the government to build your line. I want you to pick up that pen and write out a quitclaim for that company and that charter. I'm buying it."

Keats swallowed convulsively. Donovan had worked for half a dozen of the largest railroads. Maybe that was what he had come to Dondaro for — to buy out this charter for one of his former employers.

The idea of quick money swirled before Keats's eyes. The railroad had been merely a hoax, but if he could sell the charter. . . . He licked his lips. "How much?"

Ray Donovan laid a single dollar on the scarred desk top. He stepped back. He did not draw his gun, but there was a suggestion in the way his arms swung down, his fingers slightly curved, ready. "It's too much," he said. "No man alive could build that road and only a fool would try. But as long as you hold that charter, Marty might worry. I don't want her worried after I go away."

Keats stared upward at the hard, dark eyes. He told himself that he had only to refuse, but the words never formed on his lips. He picked up the pen and wrote as Donovan dictated. Then, under the man's direction, he opened the safe and got out the small ledger stock and the copy of the charter.

Donovan stuffed them into his pocket, and Wilbur Keats breathed almost freely for the first time since the man had entered the room. But Donovan was not yet through.

"Where's Friend?"

Wilbur Keats flinched. He had not expected this. "Why I . . . what do you want with Friend?"

"He murdered Bert Donovan."

The words came as a kind of shock, and Keats started to protest. But there was no need. A voice from the doorway said: "I'm here, waiting, Donovan."

Donovan stood perfectly still. Friend sounded almost amused, and the gun in his hand justified his humor. "I watched you come in here. I waited for you to come out. When you didn't, I thought maybe friend Keats might be selling out."

From the desk Wilbur Keats said quickly: "No, Sam, no. He came in here. He took the railroad charter. He. . . ."

Donovan made his turn. From the instant Sam Friend had spoken he had been readying himself, tensing his muscles. He turned, and at the same time dropped sidewise, toward the left.

As he fell, his right hand lifted the gun from the holster. He caught himself on his left, dropped on one knee, and from that crouching position he leveled his gun.

Sam Friend fired as Donovan dropped. His bullet neatly bisected the space Donovan had occupied, whipped across Keats's desk, and chunked into the wall.

He fired again. His shot was still too high to touch Donovan but it caught Wilbur Keats in the act of rising from the desk. It smashed Keats directly in the pit of the stomach.

Not until after Keats began to fall did Donovan fire. He fired once, calmly. The bullet took Friend in the chest, drilling through the heart.

Reaction squeezed Friend's trigger for a third time. The bullet seared its way across Donovan's upper arm, enough to break the skin but not enough to strike the bone. He came to his feet at once. He wasted no time on Friend who had fallen half inside the room, half on the sidewalk beyond, but he did pause long enough to examine Keats.

The man was bent over in terrible agony, not dead but dying. Donovan left him, stepped across the prostrate Friend, and went out into the street.

The sound of the shots had brought the town alive. The Box D crew gave up searching the alley behind Peggy Squires's house. They raced back toward the main street, calling to each other as they ran, John Donovan urging them on.

Ray Donovan heard them coming. He ran diagonally across toward the hotel. He had left Marty in the livery stable and the last thing he wanted was to lead the crew in that direction.

He reached the edge of the gallery, vaulted the rail, and crashed through into the lobby. Two drummers dived for shelter behind the high desk. Donovan glanced at them and forgot them. He took the steps two at a time, reached the upper hall, and ran along it. The window at the back was partly open. He thrust the sash higher and swung out.

Below him, a slanting shed roof covered the single-storied kitchen. He dropped to it and stood for a moment, staring up the darkness of the back street.

There was noise from beyond the hotel. He heard John's voice raised in a shout of anger: "He killed them both, Keats and Sam Friend!" Then a gun went off from the upper end of town. A second shot sounded, and Ray Donovan knew a quick fear.

Had they found Marty? Was she doing that firing? She hadn't wanted to stay in the livery stable. She'd wanted to come with him.

He dropped to the ground and started to run along the back street. It was darker there, the houses showing no lights. He had no real idea what time it was but it must be very late, or perhaps a better word was early, for the smell of morning freshened the air and the moon was low. Light would be showing in the east, and with daylight they would be hopelessly trapped. Whatever he did would have to be done before the sun rose again.

As he passed the mouth of the cross alley, he saw a shadow, deeper than the rest. A gun spat from the darkness, and a shrill cry rose across the town: "That's him! I saw him!" And then feet pounded down the alley toward the back street.

Donovan had swerved instinctively at the first shot, ducking around the corner of the building. He pressed close to the wall, his gun ready. He heard the feet in the alley slow. The man came to a stop, then advanced hesitantly to peer out into the street.

Donovan did not wait. He jumped sidewise, his gun spitting as he came into the alley's mouth. He saw the white blob of the man's face, then saw it vanish as the man slumped at his feet. From a hundred yards down the alley another gun leaped into life. Dust spurted up beyond Donovan. Again he sought the protection of the building corner.

He dared not continue on toward the livery stable. If Marty hadn't been discovered, he would only lead them to her. But where to go? They were coming down the alley now, made cautious by the death of the man who lay only a few feet away. From the rear of the hotel a dark figure emerged. He triggered a shot, driving the man to cover.

The building before which he stood was a one-story harness shop with a flat roof and a wooden awning supported by poles. He moved to the end away from the alley, slipped the gun into his belt, jumped lightly, caught the edge of the awning, and dragged himself up. A moment later he bellied down on the flat roof of the shop, breathing deeply through his mouth from the quick exertion. He lay thus for an instant, then rolled on his side, and reloaded his guns.

He was not panicked. This was not the first time he had been hunted through a town. Once, in Laramie, thirty men with rifles had searched the streets, sworn to hang him. He had escaped, hidden behind the glowing forge of a friendly blacksmith, and the next day, with fifty graders at his back, he had rounded up the would-be lynchers, burning their tents and driving them from the camp.

But he hadn't had Marty to worry about then, and he had no tough Irish grading crew to fall back on in the morning.

And it was very near to morning. He detected the faint suggestion of light in the east. He had so very little time.

He crawled across the roof. Its edge missed joining the building at its back, the building that faced on the main street, by a good four feet.

Below him, to the right, voices hissed directions as men moved cautiously through the alley, their boot soles scuffing as they struck an occasional stone in the red dust.

They were so close. He could have moved a few feet and spit down upon them. Yet he was alone. It seemed to him, as he crouched on the edge, calculating the jump, that he had always been alone, alone in a crowd.

He waited until the voices reached the far end of the alley, then rose, standing crouched so that his tall figure would not make an outline against the lighter sky. He made the jump, and it seemed to him that his landing on the metal roof could have been heard for miles. He eased away from the edge. A voice from the alley said sharply: "What was that?"

He waited. He heard a murmured council below, and then they moved toward the back street. He edged over the roof, working his way to the front where a wooden wall gave the false appearance of a second story.

He could not climb the wall, so he worked his way along it to the side of the building away from the alley, and peered around it at the main street below.

Light was noticeable in the eastern sky now, a fanning radiance that crept up to lessen the darkness of the distant mountains.

But he did not even glance toward the mountains. His full attention was on the street, on the big man who stood alone in the center of the ribbon of dust.

John Donovan had followed his men into the alley, snapped half a dozen shots into the darkness, and then retreated to the middle of the street. He loomed, big and powerful in the half light, waiting for them to flush the hunted man.

Below Ray, a wooden awning sheltered the

sidewalk. Some of John's men might be hidden below this awning, but it was a chance he had to take. Before him in the street stood John Donovan, the key figure in the whole fight.

He knew the impulse to shoot John down in his tracks, but the thought of Marty held his hand. John, in the final analysis, was a Donovan. John was Marty's cousin, and memories of the years in which they had grown up together came back to stay Ray Donovan's hand.

If he could disarm John without killing him, if he could force John to call off his men and get out of the country, it would be better for them all. There had been too much killing already.

He balanced himself on the roof's edge, one hand on the corner post that supported the false front, and measured the distance carefully.

Then he jumped to the slanting awning, trusting that it would bear his weight, hoping to spring from there to the street at John's side. But the awning failed to hold. Its sun-bleached planks had dry-rotted until they were little more than punk.

He came crashing down through the awning like a lead weight, dropping through a paper wall, half the structure tearing loose and falling with him to the sidewalk below.

He landed with his knees a little bent to absorb the shock. He went from there to a sitting position, so tangled with the jagged boards that for a moment it was impossible to rise.

John Donovan made his mistake then. He swung at the sound of Ray's fall, dragging his gun from its holster. He fired twice, so rapidly that he missed both times. His hammer clicked on an empty cartridge. With a curse he flung the useless gun at Ray's head, and hurled himself across the dust at the man still seated on the sidewalk.

Ray saw John coming. He was slightly dazed by the fall, but he did manage to roll sideways just as John Donovan lunged downward, knees bent, meaning to strike Ray with them, meaning to cave in Ray's chest.

John came down hard on the pile of débris from the fallen roof, jarring himself badly. But then his arms snaked out and locked about Ray's shoulders, and they rolled together into the deep dust of the street, clawing at each other like animals.

Ray was the quicker of the two. He managed to get his foot into John's stomach. A thrusting kick broke John's grip, sending him up and backward over his head. Then

Ray rolled, coming to his feet. John was a second slower in rising, but he, too, hoisted himself upright. For an instant they stood apart, breathing heavily, eyeing each other. Then John charged, head down, arms swinging in great roundhouse blows.

Ray stepped in close. He took one blow on the shoulder, another along side of his head, hard enough to make his ear ring. He hooked to the body, a right, a left, and another right.

At each blow John grunted, the wind pounded out of him, but again he locked his powerful arms around Ray, knotting the fingers in the small of Ray's back, setting his chin against Ray's chest and throwing his whole weight into an effort to bend the younger man, and at the same time to trip him.

Ray brought his knee up into John's groin. John's face twisted with pain. His grip slackened. He let go and tried to break away, but Ray was on him with the speed of a cat sensing a kill. He put a short left to the head, then buried his right under John's ribs. John tried again to clinch, but Ray shook free. Stepping backward for more room, he drove an overhand, looping right to the head, and hooked his left to the big chin.

John went down. He was on his knees, straining to lift himself into an upright position, and failing. Ray stood for an instant, gasping, mouth open, struggling to drag air into his tortured lungs. At last he stepped forward, reached down, and jerked John to his feet.

John's legs buckled. He was nearly cross-eyed, trying to focus on Ray's face. He had an idiotic grin on his lips as if the connection between his brain and his nerve system had been severed. He was as completely whipped as any man can be and still retain a semblance of consciousness, and he used that last glimmer of understanding to swing a blow toward Ray's head.

Ray released his grip and John fell on his face.

XVII

As Marty Donovan crouched in the corner stall of the livery and peered through a crack between warped sidings, she saw Ray move up the main street, keeping to the shadows. He reached Keats's office and turned in through the open door. She saw Sam Friend materialize suddenly from the shadows and step into the doorway behind Ray. Her lips opened but she choked off the urge to cry a warning. She waited. She heard the roar of their guns, but, before she could move from her hiding place, Ray ducked back into sight. He ran diagonally across the street and disappeared into the hotel.

She could only keep on waiting, now. She saw the Box D crew race into the street and she had all she could do to keep herself hidden in the stable. She was not a Donovan for nothing. No Donovan had ever stayed out of a fight since their first coming into the country.

She saw the men searching the street, and heard the shots in the alley. It was lighter now, and there stood John Donovan in the middle of the street. She heard the crash as Ray came down, breaking through the awning.

For a moment she did not quite know what had happened, and then she saw John dive forward. Ray was trapped!

No longer could she bear to stay quiet. She ran out of the stall, along the runway, and into the street. The livery was a good block away from the struggling men and she raced madly, pulling her small gun as she ran, hoping she could reach the fighters before the Box D crew came out of the alley.

In full stride, she realized suddenly that

she had forgotten Bert. In a flash it came to her that never in her whole life had she known this frantic, stabbing anxiety over Bert. Her feeling for Bert had always been maternal, very closely allied with the protective concern that Aunt Kate had entertained for her younger nephew.

But for Ray her feeling was entirely different. It came up into her throat to choke her as she ran. "Nothing must happen to him," she babbled aloud. "Nothing must happen to him, nothing." She felt that if something did happen to Ray she would no longer wish to live. She had to get there before the crew did. She had to stop the fight and hold off the crew. She was even ready to make a deal with John for the ranch if it would only save Ray. But she needed help.

She thought of the townspeople, hiding in their houses during the grim search. No, none of them would offer help. They hid, keeping out of the way while the Donovans turned their town into a bloody battleground.

There was no help, no one but herself and the small gun in her hand. She was within half a dozen doors of the fighters now. She saw Ray Donovan grab the front of John's shirt and hold him upright. She tried to call to Ray, and then a hand reached out of a doorway and halted her.

She swung around, thinking it was one of the Box D crew. She fought like a young animal to free herself, and then she realized that it was Kandee, the gambler, who held her. She stopped struggling.

Kandee's narrow, long-fingered hands had surprising strength. He held her as he might have held a small child, easily, without apparent strain.

"I've got to go." She saw Peggy Squires behind Kandee and, in the dark store beyond Peggy, the scared white faces of Peggy's girls. "I've got. . . ."

"No." Kandee's voice was even, unhurried. "Stay here, my dear. This is my job."

He passed her then, and it did not occur to her to disobey. He stepped out into the street, clearly visible in the growing morning light. He seemed very thin and tall as he moved toward the alley's mouth.

He reached Ray Donovan and spoke to him. Donovan relaxed briefly as he saw who it was. And then Donovan barked: "Get back!"

Kandee apparently didn't hear him. His pace seemed slow, but it had carried him beyond Donovan. He was standing in the middle of the street, facing the alley mouth, when the first of the Box D crew came running back.

Watching, Marty Donovan realized how very quickly things had happened. It had seemed to her as she ran along the street that ages had elapsed between the crashing sound of Donovan's fall and the appearance of the returning Box D crew.

But it had been only a little while, only the time it took for her to race along the block from the livery. The crew had been on the back street, and they had reacted slowly to the sound of the breaking awning.

They had been confused, unable to determine exactly where the noise came from, and the fight between Ray and John had been savagely silent.

But they were coming now, not hurrying, but moving steadily, led by Kemp, with Bolger at his elbow. They kept coming until they saw Kandee, standing there in the middle of the street.

They stopped for an instant, puzzled by the appearance of the gambler. But Kandee did not stop. He walked straight toward them.

"Throw down your guns," he said in his controlled voice. "It's finished, everything is finished."

"He'll be killed." Marty did not realize that she had spoken aloud. She was merely voicing her thought as it came into her head. "He acts almost as if he wants to be killed," she murmured in wonder.

She heard a half-strangled sob behind her. Peggy Squires was running, holding the shotgun awkwardly before her. And, as Peggy started down the walk, Kemp recovered from his surprise.

"To hell with it," he snarled, and the gun in his hand crashed. The bullet struck Kandee in the chest. It stopped him for an instant, the shocking power seeming to bend his slender body backward. Then he was walking ahead again, the gun in his hand talking slowly, certainly, each bullet shrewdly expended.

Kemp went down. Bolger's shot struck the gambler fully in the stomach. Kandee bent. He sank to his knees, dropping his free hand to the dust to steady himself. And he went on firing.

Ray Donovan had stood paralyzed while Kandee passed him. His big body was drugged with fatigue. At the first two shots he turned and took a step toward the alley's mouth. Then he heard Peggy Squires's running feet and twisted to see the shotgun in her hands. He reached out and seized it as she came up to his side. He leaped forward, fully alert now, shouting to Kandee to get down. Coming around the corner, he placed himself as a shield for the kneeling gambler.

He fired the shotgun from the hip, using both barrels. The shot pattern raked the alley's length, bringing startled yelps from the men in the shadows.

Two of them shot at him. A bullet tore through his right shoulder. He ignored it, dropping the shotgun and lifting his left hand revolver all in the same motion. He charged the alley and they broke before him, those who could still run.

He followed them the full length of the alley, burst into the back street, found no one in sight. It was over; he knew it with the keen feeling of experience. As long as the crew was together as a fighting unit they would stand fast. Without Kemp to lead them, scattered, hiding, their one common thought would be of escape. They would get out of town as soon as possible, singly.

He heard the hoof beats of a loping horse, another, then a third. He retraced his way along the alley. Four men were down, Kemp and Bolger dead, the other two wounded.

He walked on. Kandee had fallen over on his side. He lay curled up, his left arm under his thin face, almost like a child asleep. Peggy Squires was on her knees beside him and Marty stood at her shoulder. Donovan said: "Dead?"

Peggy Squires nodded. Donovan used the back of the hand that still held his gun to wipe his mouth. His right arm was useless. Marty saw it and started to say something, but he shook his head.

John Donovan had dragged himself to his feet and was standing in the débris from the fallen awning. He stared stupidly at Ray, as if he did not quite grasp what had happened.

Ray stooped, lifted John's gun from the dust, and deliberately loaded it with shells from his own gun. Then he tossed it at John's feet.

"You're through," he said. "Your crew's scattered. Kemp's dead. Marty and I are married. The ranch is hers."

A spark flared in John Donovan's eyes. It grew, burning.

Ray said: "It's between you and me, John. Pick up your gun. Use it."

John leaned forward as if he would obey. A sudden eager desire broke through the husk of his weariness. And then he met Ray's eyes, calm and dark and certain, and he read the purpose in them, and somehow the nerve flowed out of him like liquid from a punctured cask.

He started to turn away but Ray's voice

stopped him: "Climb your horse, John. Ride out of here. If I ever hear of you in this country again, I'll kill you."

John Donovan was too beaten to answer. Ray watched him walk slowly up the street toward the tethered horse, watched him climb heavily into the saddle, and pull his horse around, riding away slowly toward the light streak in the east, too weary and uncaring to stir the animal out of its plodding walk.

Men had appeared in the doorways and on the street, men who had hidden all during the time the Box D was searching the town. They came out slowly, sensing from past experience with such battles that the danger was past.

Donovan said curtly to the first to reach him: "Get Judge Parkman and the doctor." He was swaying a little now, unsteady on his feet, beaten out by fatigue and the loss of blood.

He looked toward the mouth of the alley where the gambler lay. Peggy Squires was still kneeling at Kandee's side. Marty Donovan stood over her. She was gazing at Kandee's still, untroubled face.

"I don't understand it." She was not talking to anyone. She was thinking aloud.

Peggy Squires said — "What is there to

understand?" — and her voice held all the bitterness of the ages. Its tone caught Marty's attention and she looked down intently at the older woman.

"You loved him, didn't you?"

Peggy Squires was genuinely surprised. "Loved him? I hardly knew him."

"But I thought. . . ."

"You thought he was my man?" She rose and bent to brush the dust from the front of her dress. "Well, he wasn't. But he was an outcast in this town, just as I'm an outcast. It was our one point in common. When he needed to talk, he came to my place, and, when he needed to hide, he came." She broke off and looked down at the still figure. "I never understood him, I guess. I didn't know until tonight that he was in love with you."

Marty Donovan gasped. "In love with me? Why, I've only spoken to him half a dozen times. He . . . he never said anything. He. . . ."

Peggy Squires was impatient. "I saw his eyes when you were being married. I know now why he helped you tonight. I didn't understand until then."

Marty caught her breath, and Peggy said in a different tone, a softer tone than anyone in Dondaro had ever heard her use: "Don't let it trouble you, baby. Kandee was dying. He knew it. He had nothing to lose. In fact, I suspect he welcomed death. So don't go building up a romantic picture of him in your memory. He was not much good, a gambler, and I imagine he dealt his share of crooked games in the past. I've seen other men like that, men who have come from decent homes, who have something twisted and wrong inside of them. He was educated. He was once what you'd call a gentlemen, I guess."

"He saved us tonight." Marty took her time studying the still face. "Without him we'd be dead. I'd like to know who he was. I'd like to know where he came from. I'd like to know his real name so that I could write to his family and tell them that he died gallantly."

"You won't know," Peggy told her. "You can be certain that he covered his tracks well. This country is filled with people like Kandee. They didn't fit back East where they belonged. They never would fit, anywhere."

Her voice hardened. "Go back to your husband and help him. Forget there ever was a Kandee. Donovan could have been another Kandee. He has the same rebellion, the same courage, and the same resentment.

He might have drifted into anything. He didn't. Something held him steady and loyal. Maybe it was you, the thought of you. Maybe it was something solid within himself."

Marty nodded slowly. "You know a lot about men, don't you?"

Peggy Squires smiled wearily. "I have to," she said, and walked away.

Marty turned and saw Donovan coming toward her. His face was drawn, gray under his heavy tan. It made his eyes seem much darker than they really were. She saw the blood on his shoulder and the awkward way his arm hung at his side, and suddenly she was afraid.

She had been grieved for Kandee, but what if it had been Ray lying there in the dust?

"Ray," she said, as if she had been long away and was just coming back, "Ray, darling." And she was running to him and feeling his good arm close about her protectively.

"What, Marty?" he said, and sounded surprised even through the dullness of his fatigue. "What?"

"I love you," she whispered against his shoulder, "love you, love you with all my heart."

It wasn't a lie. She knew. She had learned something in the last few tortured hours. She had thought that the human heart could love only one person, but she knew now that there were many kinds of love. Like the tenderness she still held for Bert, sealed off in its little niche, warm and meaningful. And the sorrow she felt for Kandee, for his wasted years, for his lonely death. But above all others there arose the feeling she had for this man with whom she hoped to spend the rest of her life. She lifted her head and offered her lips for his kiss.

ABOUT THE AUTHOR

Todhunter Ballard was born in Cleveland, Ohio. He was graduated with a bachelor's degree from Wilmington College in Ohio, having majored in mechanical engineering. His early years were spent working as an engineer before he began writing fiction for the magazine market. As W.T. Ballard he was one of the regular contributors to *The Black Mask* magazine along with Dashiell Hammett and Erle Stanley Gardner. Although Ballard published his first Western story in *Cowboy Stories* in 1936, the same year he married Phoebe Dwiggins, it wasn't until *Two-Edged Vengeance* (1951) that he produced his first Western novel. Ballard later claimed that Phoebe, following their marriage, had co-written most of his fiction with him and perhaps this explains, in part, his memorable female characters. Ballard's Golden Age as a Western author came in the 1950s and extended to the early 1970s.

Incident at Sun Mountain (1952), *West of Quarantine* (1953), and *High Iron* (1953) are among his finest early historical titles, published by Houghton Mifflin. After numerous traditional Westerns for various publishers, Ballard returned to the historical novel in *Gold in California!* (1965) which earned him a Spur Award from the Western Writers of America. It is a story set during the Gold Rush era of the 'Forty-Niners. However, an even more panoramic view of that same era is to be found in Ballard's *magnum opus, The Californian* (1971), with its contrasts between the *Californios* and the emigrant gold-seekers, and the building of a freight line to compete with Wells Fargo. It was in his historical fiction that Ballard made full use of his background in engineering combined with exhaustive historical research. However, these novels are also character-driven, gripping a reader from first page to last with their inherent drama and the spirit of adventure so true of those times.

The employees of Thorndike Press hope you have enjoyed this Large Print book. All our Thorndike, Wheeler, and Kennebec Large Print titles are designed for easy reading, and all our books are made to last. Other Thorndike Press Large Print books are available at your library, through selected bookstores, or directly from us.

For information about titles, please call:
(800) 223-1244

or visit our Web site at:
http://gale.cengage.com/thorndike

To share your comments, please write:
Publisher
Thorndike Press
10 Water St., Suite 310
Waterville, ME 04901